MEGAN MILES

©2024 by Megan Miles

Legacy of Grace Publishing

All rights reserved. No part of this publication may be reproduced, scanned, uploaded, stored in a retrieval system, or transmitted, in any form or by any means, electronic, mechanical, photocopying, recording, or otherwise, without the prior written permission of the publisher.

Printed in the United States of America

Paperback ISBN: 979-8-9900575-0-0

Ebook ISBN: 979-8-9900575-1-7

Scripture quotations are from the King James Version of the Bible.

This is a work of historical fiction: any references to historical events, real people, or real places are used fictitiously. Other names, characters, places, and events are products of the author's imagination, and any resemblances to actual events or places or persons, living or dead, is entirely coincidental.

Cover design by Miblart.com

To my parents, Matt and Theresa
Your support allowed me to see my writing dreams come true

CHAPTER 1

As Evelyn's eyes flickered open to take in the early morning light, visions of colorful silks and lace twirled through her thoughts. Couples danced across a polished floor beneath large electrical chandeliers. Every inch of her skin tingled with the memory of strong but gentle hands resting on her waist. Piercing blue eyes captivated hers as they stepped in time to the live orchestra, but when she blinked, she was staring at the wooden beams stretched across her peaked ceiling. She would have believed it to be an enchanting dream if not for the leftover nervous excitement still quivering in her belly.

Drawing herself upright, Evelyn dared to peek past the end of her bed. The discarded pile of light blue chiffon and satin on her wooden floors was a sure reminder that every blissful moment was, in fact, a memory. She flopped back on her pillow, her chest deflating with a deep sigh.

A brief, electrifying kiss under a floral trellis seared into her thoughts, and heat flooded her cheeks. Burying her face in her hands, she turned into her pillow to let out a girlish squeal. Daniel Prindall, heir of a million-dollar factory enterprise and frequenter of her daydreams since girlhood, had kissed her, little Evelyn Macaree from 24th Street.

She lay still in her bed for several minutes, letting more memories of the night wash over her—memories she wanted to relive every second of every day so she would never forget them. The live music reverberating through the tall, arching ceilings, filling the room with life and energy. Daniel assigning himself the position by her side for most of the evening, doting on her with plenty of refreshments between their dances. The gazes of the other girls along the wall, their whispers following them in wonder of who she was, and for one night, she was someone else entirely.

As the sun drifted upward in the sky, the light jabbed into her eyes too brightly to ignore. She dragged herself upright again, casting one last wistful glance at her gown on the floor. The feeling of pure bliss that made her chest swell with ecstasy faded away, leaving behind a gaping ache at the thought of the fairytale night evaporating into mere reminiscence forever.

Evelyn climbed out of bed to gather the dress into her arms, tendrils of the perfume she had worn the night before escaping from the folds of the fabric to offer her one last tangible reminder of the night. After opening the lid of the trunk at the end of the bed, she folded the dress with care on top of the other garments tucked inside. She would have to return the dress to her friend Edith whenever the chance arose, along with an enormous thank you for the outfit and the evening.

A pair of heels lay abandoned on the floor, but when she picked them up, she paused to run her thumb over the scuffs caused by her hasty climb up the lattice to her window. For the first time, a bit of guilt pricked at her chest. Never before had she so blatantly gone against her stepmother's wishes, but with all of the wonderful memories, she could only feel guilty about it for a second. There was no good reason for her step-mother to forbid her from attending the party other than pure jealousy that Edith had invited Evelyn to such a prominent function.

After closing the trunk to conceal the only evidence of her disobedience, she focused on getting around for the day. The simple, worn wool of the skirt she pulled on paled in comparison to the luxurious feel of the satin against her skin, and the pleated gray blouse covered her ghostly collarbones that had seen the light of day for the first time in her life.

She sighed as she sat in the broken dining chair that served as a vanity chair. Staring past the rust spots on the aging mirror, she pinned her dark waves into a conservative bun on top of her head. She paused with hairpins clasped between her lips as more memories of the night surfaced. The way Edith had curled and arranged Evelyn's dark tresses resembled the Greek goddess statues in the Prindall's grand entryway. Her rouge cheeks and colored lips had turned her soft face doll-like. She had never seen herself look so fashionable or... beautiful.

She reached into the high collar of her shirt to draw out her familiar cross necklace, but her fingertips only found bare skin. Fear tightened her throat as she groped around her neck.

"Mother's necklace," she breathed into the quiet room.

When had she worn it last? She wore it into the ball, even if Edith claimed it was too plain and stiff to wear to a party. But had she still worn it while she undressed in the darkness of her room? Evelyn rose from the vanity to search the floor, but her frenzied search under the furnishings proved it was nowhere to be found.

She sat back on her heels with a groan. She must have lost it somewhere between the estate ballroom and her bedroom. Several miles and hours stretched between the two.

She swallowed as she leaned against the bed. Was this her punishment from God for going against her stepmother? The loss of her own mother's necklace felt too cruel, especially considering that this was her first infraction.

"Evelyn!" A shrill call cut through her closed bedroom door.

Evelyn buried her face in her hands, knowing without being told she was late for assisting the housekeeper with breakfast. As she stood to her feet, she gathered her emotions to tuck them away behind a complaisant veil. Descending the two flights of stairs to the ground level of their narrow townhouse, she tried to erase all thoughts of the night from her mind. Upon reaching the base of the stairs, she straightened her shoulders under her stepmother's impatient gaze.

Prudence stood with her fists planted on her corset-narrowed waist. Even if it was several years behind the current style, her blue dress with black ruffled trim and leg-of-mutton sleeves made her look every bit their middle-class status, if not a bit more.

"Lottie has been preparing breakfast on her own," Prudence snapped with a lift of her chin. "Where have you been?"

"I'm sorry. I overslept." Evelyn lowered her eyes. If the housekeeper was in such desperate need of help, where were Dahlia and Florence? "I'll help her finish."

Evelyn made her way through the dining room toward the kitchen. Both of her stepsisters sat at their places on one side of the dining table, their steely gazes trailing her as she passed through. In the kitchen, she found Lottie dishing cream of wheat into four porcelain bowls.

"I'm sorry for oversleeping." Evelyn grabbed the tray of jams and fixings already prepared.

"I'd oversleep too if I climbed to my room well after midnight," Lottie muttered under her breath without pausing the wooden spoon in her hand.

Evelyn froze, pressing the tray into her stomach. "Do you think anyone else heard?"

Lottie pursed her lips as she carried the bowls to the dining room. Evelyn followed behind the housekeeper with the tray, her cheeks warming. Neither woman said anything as they set the food before Evelyn's stepfamily.

Dahlia sniffed as she looked down at her bowl. "Cream of wheat? Father got eggs."

"This will fill out your bones just the same." Lottie kept her words light enough to not offend, but a firm undertone discouraged argument. "I have linens to wash. Excuse me."

Prudence frowned at Lottie, but the housekeeper disappeared before Dahlia could complain further. Evelyn slid into the seat next to her stepmother and began to top her cream of wheat in silence. As she flicked a glob of jelly off the spoon into her bowl, her mind couldn't help going to the arrangement of pastries and finger foods offered at the party. Daniel had selected a plate of options to share as an intermission to their dancing, asking if he met her tastes with his choices. She would have eaten cod liver oil if he had offered it.

She was unaware of the smile lifting her lips until her stepsister gave an indignant sniff.

"Someone is in a good mood," Florence commented as she picked up her spoon, but her glowering gaze caused Evelyn to tense. "And here I was assuming you were late to breakfast because you were sulking in your room over missing that ball you begged all week for." She lifted one delicate eyebrow. The frizzy, auburn curls that framed her haughty face had fallen from her floppy attempt at a loose Gibson girl pompadour style.

Evelyn held her gaze, trying to decide if she knew something or if she was simply baiting her. Deciding to err on the side of caution, she turned her focus to her stepmother. "Where is Papa?"

"He's already at work. You would have known that if you were up earlier." Prudence didn't spare Evelyn a glance as she sprinkled brown sugar into her bowl.

How long did Prudence plan to hold that over her head? Giving up on conversation, Evelyn focused on stirring her cream of wheat. No matter how hard she tried not to, her mind returned to the events of last night. Nothing could seem to dim the warmth that spread in her with one thought of Daniel. The memory of his smile evaporated any of her displeasure.

Breakfast continued in a quiet fashion, with her stepfamily occasionally commenting on the day's plans to each other. As always, they intentionally left Evelyn out of the conversation, allowing her to remain blissfully in her thoughts and memories.

As Dahlia laid her napkin next to her empty bowl and politely excused herself, Evelyn glanced at her half-full bowl that she had been stirring more than eating.

Prudence stared down her narrow nose at Evelyn's food. "Are you going to let food go to waste?"

Before Evelyn could formulate a reply, the stairs creaked. Her heart leaped into her throat as she rose from the table and dashed down the hall.

"Dahlia?" She called up to the second floor, hoping and praying her stepsister hadn't gone any higher.

"I knew it!" Dahlia shrieked from the third floor.

"Leave my things alone!" Evelyn grabbed her skirt to take the stairs two at a time, but it was too late.

Dahlia came out of the attic room, the ballgown in her hands.

"You dug in my trunk." Evelyn clenched her fists.

"Where did you get this?" Dahlia shook the dress at Evelyn. "You can't afford anything like this. That rotten friend of yours gave it to you and took you to the ball."

"Give it back!" Evelyn reached in vain for the dress as Dahlia snatched it away.

"What is the meaning of all this noise?" Prudence barked from the ground-floor hall.

Evelyn lowered her head, hiding her shaking fists within the folds of her skirt.

"Evelyn defied your authority." Dahlia raised the dress as evidence for Prudence to see. "I found this in her room."

"Please give it back to me." Evelyn kept her voice even and quiet. "It's Edith's dress, and I can't repay her if it's ruined."

"I have half a mind to tear it up for your insolence," Dahlia hissed.

"Give her the dress."

Evelyn jumped at her stepmother's voice, and she turned to find Prudence now standing on the second floor with them. Prudence's thin lips were drawn in a taunt line, her eyes like bone-chilling ice.

Dahlia frowned. "But Mother—"

"We don't damage other people's property we aren't prepared to pay for," Prudence stated without a change in expression.

Evelyn swallowed as Dahlia shoved the dress into her arms.

"But she—" Dahlia whined until a raised hand from her mother cut her off.

"Did you go to the party, Evelyn?" Prudence asked.

Evelyn lowered her gaze. "Yes, ma'am."

Prudence's hand slapped across Evelyn's face. Still gripping the dress in one hand, Evelyn stumbled back a step and put her other hand to her stinging cheek. She turned a gaping expression to her unmoved stepmother.

"That's for your disobedience," Prudence spoke with a steely tone unchanged from before. "You knew my orders."

Evelyn swallowed down mounting frustration. "I don't understand why you said no to begin with. The outfit cost you nothing. We had no other plans. Edith picked me up. Edith did everything, and it was her invitation. It was a harmless, fun night." As Prudence narrowed her eyes, Evelyn rushed on, "I never disobey you. I always do whatever you ask. Why couldn't I have one night for myself?"

Prudence grabbed her arm, causing her to wince. "Because I'm your mother, and I told you not to go."

"You're not my mother."

This time she expected—and was prepared for—the slap to the same cheek. Tears burned her eyes despite her attempts to hold them at bay.

"Your father chose me as the woman of this house, and whether you like it or not, what I say will be the final word as long as you are under this roof," Prudence hissed. "I don't need a reason for my orders."

"But there was nothing wrong with it!"

"Nothing wrong?" She let out a bark of a laugh. "Girls like you don't belong at such affairs. Do you think one rich friend makes you an expert? Masquerading in a world where you don't belong will do nothing for you but fill your head with useless fantasies."

Evelyn kept her gaze on the hallway rug. Rebuttals filtered through her mind, but no doubt Prudence would have a quick answer for anything she said.

Prudence leaned closer. "What happens if a rich man decides to seduce you and have his way with you for sport?" Her whispered words left a chill down Evelyn's spine. She tried to pull away, but Prudence grabbed her arm again. "You're naive, Evelyn. You would believe every word coming off his honey lips and go along with it, ruining yourself forever. Humiliating your father's good name."

Evelyn closed her eyes as she turned her face away from her stepmother.

Prudence released her arm before whirling away, her skirts flaring and rustling. "Your father will hear about this the second he returns this evening. In the meantime, I'll inform Lottie you will clean up breakfast."

As Prudence stomped down the stairs, followed by a smug Dahlia, Evelyn hugged the satin dress to her chest. Her fingertips brushed her lips, and the feeling of Daniel's stolen kiss flashed through her memory again, sending a blanket of shame to smother the warm feelings from before. Had she almost fallen for an ill-intended seduction? Maybe she should thank the Lord that Edith rushed her home before anything more could take place in the garden.

Feeling numb except for the stinging in her cheek, she trudged up the steps to her room to return the dress to the trunk.

On her way back to the dining room, she passed Florence in the hall. Even if Florence had managed to stay out of the hallway drama, she didn't miss the opportunity to watch Evelyn's defeated walk with a faint sneer. Lottie met her with a sympathetic look before leaving the kitchen.

In the kitchen alone, Evelyn took a few even breaths before gathering the dirtied dishes, and she scraped what remained of her uneaten breakfast into the garbage bucket.

As she washed the dishes, her stomach knotted itself in so many twists she feared she would be sick. Had she narrowly avoided entangling herself in something compromising with Daniel? Were his intentions throughout the dreamlike night far different than she imagined? No matter how hard she tried, she couldn't believe it.

No matter what she envisioned, she couldn't make herself regret going to the party. Maybe that was even more reason for her to feel ashamed, but it was the best night of her life. How could she regret it?

"Honour thy father and thy mother."

The words taught to her since childhood echoed through her mind like an unwanted reminder. Perhaps she was in the wrong for not feeling ashamed for disobeying her stepmother. Her fingers went to her throat in search of the cross necklace, only to remember she'd lost it. Instead, she clasped her hands against her chest.

Lord, please forgive me for my dishonesty and disobedience. I won't let it happen again.

As she plunged her hands into soapy dishwater, she blew out a breath. The night before had been a wonderful, breathtaking dream, but it had been just that, a momentary dream. For years growing up, she had been infatuated with Daniel, and at least for a moment, she felt what it was like to be in his arms, whether his intentions for the night had been pure or not.

In the end, nothing happened. Now she had returned to reality, and nothing was more real than washing her stepfamily's dishes.

As she stacked the bowls and utensils in their appropriate cupboards, Evelyn had to admit to herself that maybe Prudence was right to a point: Daniel's world of glamor and money was out of her reach. She looked down at the front of her skirt and shirt riddled with water stains, and she tried to picture Daniel at her side in all of his finery. It was an impossible image to conjure.

"Evelyn! Are you about done yet?" Prudence's shrill call drifted from somewhere else in the house.

Evelyn closed her eyes and leaned on the kitchen counter. Daniel's world was outside of her reach, but remaining under Prudence's thumb was not a place she wanted to be either. Maybe her time would be better spent finding someone who could sweep her away from this house. A husband who would provide for her needs with love and carry her far away from her stepfamily.

That was a dream she was willing to forget Daniel for.

CHAPTER 2

*E*velyn closed the attic door on Florence's boisterous piano lessons.

"Why did you sneak me up here?" Edith asked as she sat on the edge of the bed. Unlike Evelyn's faded quilt, Edith's red cotton dress stood out like a freshly bloomed poppy.

Evelyn rubbed her arms, unable to look her friend in the eyes. "I don't think my stepmother would be happy you're here."

"They found out, didn't they?" Edith groaned. "I'm so sorry. Now I don't know if my news will compensate for your misfortune."

"What news?"

Evelyn sank onto the bed, but Edith nearly knocked her over as she grabbed Evelyn's shoulder with a gasp. She forced Evelyn to turn her face toward the sunlight streaming from the single window. "Evelyn! Your cheek is all red!"

Evelyn touched the tender spot on her face. Apparently, her attempt to hide the redness with powder had failed. "I'm all right."

Edith held her by her shoulders, piercing her with a sober

look intensified by the sharpness of her blue eyes. "Did your stepmother do this to you?"

"I'm all right," she repeated, brushing off Edith's delicate gloved hands. "What was your news?"

Edith crossed her arms, her stern expression hardening the edges of her soft, doll-like face.

"Come on." Evelyn smiled as she tried to tug her arms apart. "You can't withhold it from me now."

A smile twitched at Edith's mouth. "I'm not through worrying about that mark on your face, but I also can't keep this in for another second. Guess who won't stop going on about this captivating girl he met last night?"

Evelyn's eyes widened, and she sat back in surprise. "What?"

Edith's whole countenance changed as she squealed and grabbed Evelyn's hands. "My brother won't stop talking about you. Of course, he doesn't realize who you are, but wait until I tell him."

"Are you sure he's talking about me?" Evelyn stiffened. Daniel found her captivating?

"I'm sorry, was there another girl he danced with all night? You didn't give any other girls a chance," Edith teased. "At the breakfast table this morning, he declared that he was determined to find out who you were. I—"

Evelyn gripped Edith's hands to cut off her bubbling words. "Did you tell him the truth? Please tell me you didn't."

Edith smirked. "Not yet. I'm enjoying his torment. I also wanted to warn you before he comes barging through your door in his lover's frenzy."

She choked on a gasp, her cheeks blazing with heat. "That's... It's not... Please don't use that kind of speech. We aren't lovers. It was one party. Nothing happened."

"'Nothing happened.' I supposed that's why he had your lipstick on his mouth when I swept you away at midnight." Edith gave her a knowing look.

"I-it was one brief kiss." Evelyn withdrew her hands from Edith and wrapped them around her middle. Her stepmother's words about him wanting to take advantage of her rang through her mind, making her feel dirty all over again.

But if what Edith said was true, it seemed he didn't view her as just another girl to have a good time with. Was it possible the night had been as alluring for Daniel as it was for her? She had assumed that kind of party was a nightly occurrence for someone of his station. How had she stood out to him when he had plenty of eligible high-society women casting themselves at his feet?

A new fear squeezed Evelyn's heart. "You have to swear that you won't tell him who I am."

"Whyever not? He's dying to find you!"

"You can't," Evelyn pressed. "If he finds out the truth…"

"What truth? You're an amazing woman. I almost think you're too good for my stuffy brother."

"No, I'm not. He's an heir to everything your father owns. I'm… a factory manager's daughter. One of *his* factory manager's daughters at that. I shouldn't have been there last night, and I wouldn't have been invited if it wasn't for our friendship."

Edith's shoulders drooped. "But Ev, I think he really likes you. I've never heard him talk about a girl like this before."

"The girl he met last night was an entirely different person because of your skillful hand and beautiful wardrobe." She motioned to her plain gray attire next to Edith's vibrant color. "The real me will only disappoint his expectations. I think it's best for both of us to keep last night a beautiful dream unspoiled by reality."

Even though she said the words without wavering, her heart sank after they left her lips. Drawing her shoulders straight to keep from losing her resolve, she stood to open the trunk at the end of the bed. "Speaking of which, I need to return this to you. I'm sorry about the shoes. I'll repay you for them."

Edith sighed as she accepted the dress. "They're a little too small for me anyway. Keep them."

"Are you sure?" Evelyn brushed her thumb over a scuff on the heel. It felt wrong to keep her friend's expensive possessions without paying for them, but rejecting the offer would mean losing her only physical reminder of that wonderful night. Knowing Daniel's feelings made every memory that much sweeter.

Edith covered Evelyn's hand with her own. "I'm sure." Her soft smile seemed to relay that she understood what the shoes meant to Evelyn.

"Thank you," Evelyn whispered.

"I should leave before your stepsister's lesson finishes and they realize I'm here." Edith started toward the door but then paused. "I almost forgot. Did you lose your necklace last night?"

Evelyn's hand went to her bare throat. "Did you find it?"

"No, but Daniel did. He's determined to return it to the owner himself. Since you don't want to see him, I'll try to retrieve it for you."

"Thank you. I'm glad it's not lost forever. I'll walk you to the door."

Together, the girls descended the stairs, Florence's pounding on the piano covering the creaking steps.

At the front door, Evelyn paused to hug Edith. "Thank you again for last night, Edith. You're a true friend."

"I'm only sorry it brought you trouble." Edith brushed her fingers near the red mark on Evelyn's cheek. "Take care of yourself."

Evelyn waved her off before shutting the door. She slipped back up to her room, and after closing the door again, she flopped on her bed. Daniel's handsome face filled her mind as she reflected on Edith's claims that he was enamored with her. How could that be true?

She had befriended Edith shortly after her mother's death at the young age of eight. They hadn't hired Lottie yet, so after school, she always joined her father at his factory for the remainder of his workday. One day, the factory owner, Mr. Prindall, came to inspect operations, and his curious little daughter had joined him. Too young to understand social construct, Edith and Evelyn became fast friends, frequently visiting each other's homes ever since.

It was Edith's thirteenth birthday when Evelyn first laid eyes on her college brother, Daniel. Only seventeen himself, he seemed so grown up and manly to the girl with little experience around boys. From then on, Evelyn looked for him when she visited Edith at her estate home. She dreamed of him noticing her someday, but she also knew it would remain a dream, never to be reality. If her younger self knew he was searching for her now, she would have fainted away.

She rolled on her side and nibbled at her thumbnail. Was it possible Daniel was enamored enough to want to marry her? The absurd thought made her breath catch. How many nights had she knelt by this very bed, asking the Lord to send her a prince charming to sweep her far away?

"Evelyn!"

She closed her eyes as Prudence's call rattled through her door.

She would give anything for a man like Daniel to take her away. By his rich, powerful side, she would never have to answer to another one of her stepfamily's demands or take another painful blow from Prudence's abusive hand. In his household, she would never be expected to do work that wasn't required of her supposed sisters. She would never sleep alone, with only prayers to comfort her aching heart.

As Prudence called again, she sat up with a sigh. Why was she giving in to those fanciful thoughts? She was saving herself a lot of heartache by swearing Edith to silence. Things might seem rosy now, but what would it feel like if Daniel was disgusted by the truth of her identity?

"Evelyn, don't make me call again!"

She was Evelyn Macaree, daughter of a factory manager and slave to her stepfamily's every beck and call.

Evelyn dragged herself out of bed and opened her door in time to see her stepmother marching up the stairs.

"I'm sorry. What did you need?" Evelyn tried to look as apologetic as possible to avoid another confrontation.

Prudence planted her hands on her narrowed waist. "Lottie is still at the store, but it's time for tea."

She waved her hand in a circle as if those words alone should spark action in Evelyn. Biting her tongue on a snide remark—that all three of them had hands that could pour their own cups of tea—she descended the stairs.

Prudence caught her arm as she passed. "Don't make things worse for yourself. I'm reporting your behavior to your father tonight," she hissed.

"I didn't say anything," Evelyn argued, freeing her arm from her stepmother's vice grip.

Prudence pointed her long fingernail inches from Evelyn's face. "I see the look in your eyes."

Evelyn turned away from the accusing finger and hurried down the remainder of the stairs. Even when biting her tongue, her compliant obedience wasn't enough.

Evelyn busied herself with making tea in the kitchen, burying her feelings like she learned to do years ago, and once Lottie returned, she helped her prepare dinner. Anything to stay out of her stepfamily's way for the remainder of the day.

When they finally sat down to eat their evening meal, she glanced at her father's empty chair at the head of the table. Prudence said nothing as she and her daughters began to eat. Evelyn lowered her head to thank the Lord for the blessing of the food and to pray for her father.

Silverware scraping on porcelain filled the silence around the table. Dahlia and Florence whispered to each other throughout the meal, but no other conversation attempts were made, to Evelyn's relief. As soon as she finished eating, she went to the kitchen to prepare a plate for her father. She placed it on the stove and made sure the coals were still burning to keep it warm. When she turned to the dishes in the sink, Lottie waved her out of the way.

"You should relax with your family," Lottie stated as she plunged her hands into the water. "I'm the one paid to clean."

"Spending time with them is the last thing I want to do right now." Evelyn sighed, leaning on a nearby counter.

"Then you might enjoy escaping to your room with a parcel that came today," Lottie whispered, a smile sneaking up her stiff lips.

Evelyn's eyes widened. "Is it finally here?"

"Check the table in the entry. I didn't mention something sooner because I feared your stepmother was in the mood to take it away."

"Thank you!" Evelyn pecked the housekeeper on her rosy cheek before rushing from the kitchen.

As promised, the brown parcel waited for her next to the rest of the day's mail on the table by their front door. Unable to wait for the safety of her room, she tore into the paper until the beautiful cover of the latest Howard Knightly Adventures book was revealed. "Peril on the Cliffs of Moher by August Cates" glittered in gold lettering at the top, and below was a drawn picture of Howard Knightly standing on the edge of a cliff, locked in a battle of strength with a masked man.

Hugging the book to her chest like her stepmother would come any minute to snatch it from her, Evelyn hurried upstairs to her room. Once in the solace of her own space, she curled up on the chair tucked into the corner of the room and stared at the beautiful book in the light of her oil lamp. Cracking open the stiff cover, she inhaled the heavenly scent of fresh paper and ink. On the first page of chapter one, the prose transported her to the lush countryside of Ireland. She could almost hear the wind whistling in her ears, the fog leaving a mist in her curls.

She followed on Howard's heels as he explored the mystic isles in search of his allusive foe, Dr. Draper. The fiendish villain had found more people to terrorize, and Howard was once again determined to put an end to his schemes.

Only the slamming of the front door pulled her out of the distant world. She lowered her book as another door somewhere on the first floor closed. Probably her father's study. In a flash, the excitement of adventure melted away into dread. Tucking a ribbon into the book to keep her place, she left it on her bed and stood in the doorway to listen.

Seconds and then minutes ticked by without any further noise. Was Prudence speaking with him, or had she forgotten? The latter seemed unlikely. When she was about to return to her book, the door below opened and shut again.

"Evelyn! Your father wishes to speak with you." Prudence's voice rang through the house with a smug undertone.

Bracing herself against whatever was to come, Evelyn descended the stairs. Prudence stood in the hallway, arms crossed, but Evelyn kept her chin up as she stepped past her stepmother to enter her father's study.

"Hello, Papa." She closed the door behind her to prevent Prudence's interference.

Everything in the study was as it always had been, as far as she could remember. Bookcases lined every wall except the one with the door, filling the room with the comforting smell of book-binding glue, leather, and old paper. Edwin Macaree sat at the dark oak desk in the center of the room, his graying head bent over the ledger on the desktop. The overstuffed leather chair across from his desk beckoned her to curl up between its comforting arms and spend the rest of the evening in the presence of her father like she had done for years after her mother passed. They didn't talk much. Each was often absorbed in their own book, but it was the simplicity of each other's presence that they needed. When had she stopped doing that?

Edwin finally looked up at his daughter, his fork poised over the dinner plate she had prepared. "You went to the party Prudence told you not to attend."

She lowered her gaze at the quiet disappointment in her father's voice, and the chasm that had grown between them resurfaced, reminding her why she stopped coming to her father's study. It loomed between them, a dark presence with dark eyes that now ruled his home.

"You're a young woman. Why does your stepmother still need to reprimand you like a child?"

She winced at her father's words but gave no reply. What answer could she give that he wouldn't immediately rebut?

"I know that it can be hard to respect Prudence since she isn't your mother." His knowing gaze pierced her heart. Prudence must have told him the complete story, word for word. "However, she is the woman I chose as my wife. That makes her the woman of this house and the authority I expect you to respect as long as you live here. I'm sure she had a reason for not permitting you to go."

"Yes, Father," Evelyn whispered, letting her gaze fall to the Persian rug that filled much of the floor space.

"This act of rebellion surprises me, Evelyn. I know you were raised better than that. See that it doesn't happen again. You're dismissed."

She looked up to ask him about his day, but his focus had already returned to the book before him. He turned the page filled with tables and numbers, his weary eyes skimming over the accounts. The chasm seemed to elongate the room, alienating her from his attention. Swallowing her disappointment, she excused herself, and she cast one last look at her father as she closed the door.

He returned his fork to his partially eaten plate and rubbed his forehead. The dark circles under his eyes and creases at the corner of his mouth aged his handsome face. When had his hair become more gray than brown?

Taking the stairs back to her bedroom slowly, Evelyn tried to remember the last time her father hadn't looked tired. It must have been before her mother became sick. A time long gone, but she could still remember it. Back then, her father's eyes shone with life and love every time he beheld his wife and daughter.

He didn't escape to his work every minute of the day either. He rushed home in time for family dinner, and their weekends often consisted of town outings like picnics in the park. Even if it was only the three of them, she remembered a house bursting at the seams with laughter and life.

In the attic doorway, she stopped and once again brushed her fingers over the spot on her chest where her mother's necklace was supposed to rest. Tears misted over her eyes. Tears for the joy her mother took with her when she passed. Tears for the father she felt she no longer had. Tears for the weight of living under her stepfamily's domain.

With a heavy heart far different from the one she woke with, Evelyn changed into her nightgown and braided her dark waves for the night. Perhaps it was a bit early for bed, but she was too tired to care. She opened her nightstand drawer and pulled out a frame tucked away from her stepfamily's prying eyes.

It was the first and only family picture she had ever taken. Her father sat with her mother standing beside him, her hand on his shoulder. The simple gesture and the softness of her father's young face exhibited the affection between the couple. Evelyn sat on her father's knee, an impossibly large bow holding back her curls. Her face was a matching image of her mother's beauty, though much rounder from youth. Even though none of them smiled, her mother's bright eyes showed her inner joy that echoed through her family.

Evelyn sunk to her knees by her bed, holding the picture to her chest. She closed her eyes and bowed her head as her mother taught her in her earliest memories.

"Dear Heavenly Father..." She hesitated. Her usual prayers of thanksgiving and requests for a blessing on behalf of those she loved died on her tongue.

Her gaze drifted to the dark sky outside her window. "Father, please forgive me for my sin of disobedience last night. I know I was wrong, but..." She closed her eyes again as tears misted her vision. "But I was so happy. I'm trying to be content and patient, but I don't know how much longer I can bear it here. Please send someone, even if it's not Daniel, to sweep me far away from here. I want to be loved, Father, please."

CHAPTER 3

*E*velyn spread the plated desserts in front of the half-empty pie pans so that the picnickers would have clear options to choose from. As she reached for the pie server to add a few more slices of apple pie to the array, someone gently touched her on the back.

"Evelyn, dear, your work is very appreciated," the pastor's wife, Claire, murmured. "But I think you should get your own plate while there's still something to have. The Spencer children are eyeing the table for a third time."

Evelyn smiled as she straightened. "I'll finish putting out these desserts, and then I'll fix my plate. Think you can hold the Spencers off that long?"

Claire patted her shoulder. "I'll try my best, but no promises."

"Tell them pie is ready, and that should divert their attention."

Evelyn hurried to cut and lay out the apple pie. She escaped the dessert table in time for the five Spencer boys to stampede.

As she wandered over to the table containing the main courses, her gaze skimmed the park that the after-church picnickers had taken over. The women had brought out their biggest and best hats to fit the occasion, and thankfully the impossibly high piles of feathers and bows had little to fear from the wind. The picnic's success was self-evident by the happy faces and many empty plates as the picnickers stood or lounged in groups to converse and relax in the warm sun.

Evelyn dished an array of fruits onto her plate along with a small piece of the meatloaf Claire brought. Adding one of Lottie's rolls to the edge of the plate, she turned to find a place to enjoy her food. Her father stood nearby in the shade with several other men in their Sunday best suits and straw hats. His hands bobbed about animatedly as he talked, and for a moment, even a small smile tugged at his lips.

Evelyn turned in the opposite direction to find her stepsisters sitting at one of the picnic tables with several of their friends. The girls' giggles rose above the other chatter. Dahlia met her gaze before turning away with a dismissive lift of her shoulder.

After confirming that her stepmother was busy with her own group as well, Evelyn retrieved her book bag from under the food table and headed toward a quieter section of trees. A large tree practically begged her to come and relax, offering the perfect root as a seat. Evelyn sighed in relief as she plopped onto the root and freed her feet of her pinching church shoes.

Sneaking a glance around to ensure there was no one near enough to think her rude, she pulled the Howard Knightly book out of her bag. With a strawberry in hand, she flipped to where she had left off the night before.

Howard Knightly raced on horseback across a lush green Irish field, the whirl of an engine dangerously close behind him. The devious villain, Dr. Draper, pursued Howard in his newly invented flying machine.

Howard had stumbled upon the barn where Dr. Draper was working on his machine, something he hoped to use to smuggle stolen silver to England without navy patrollers catching on. When Howard attempted to throw a wrench in his plans, quite literally, Dr. Draper chased him down.

Howard urged the horse on with his heels, his fists tangled in the horse's mane. Sweat beaded on his forehead and around his collar, but his clear blue eyes glinted with rugged determination.

Uninvited, the image of a different pair of clear blue eyes flashed through Evelyn's mind. They glinted with a different kind of rugged determination as his lips descended on hers.

Evelyn covered her face with the book as her cheeks flamed. Why did Daniel's handsome face keep popping up in her mind at the most unwanted times? Was she still thirteen?

"Excuse me, miss?"

Evelyn jumped at the deep voice. She lowered the book to find a man standing a yard or two away, his hands stuffed deep in the pockets of his brown dress pants. He smiled at her beneath the shade of his straw Panama hat. Her mind scrambled to place him, but she was certain he wasn't from church. At least not a regular attendee.

"I couldn't help but notice the book you're reading." He removed one hand from his pocket to motion toward it. "Are you enjoying it?"

"Oh, definitely." She slid her ribbon back into the book so she wouldn't lose her place. "If you like adventure stories, this is one of the best series." She wasn't about to tell him that she had lost her focus to a daydream while reading one of the most intense scenes, but that wasn't the book's fault.

He leaned on the tree and pushed his hat back to show more of his dark brown eyes. A lock of mousy brown hair escaped his hat to fall over his tan forehead. "So you enjoy the whole series, then?"

She hesitated, unsure what to think of the invasive stranger before her. His smile seemed warm enough. "I own them all, and this is the latest." She held the book up so he could clearly view the cover. "Mr. Cates has a wonderful way of transporting you to faraway lands. The adventure is so thrilling that I feel like I hold my breath through the whole book."

He chuckled. "You make me want to pick it up right now."

"Are you a reader?"

"I dabble when time allows." He shrugged one shoulder. "I don't doubt, thanks to your passionate words, that you enjoy this series, but I have to believe it can't be without flaws. Is there anything you don't like about it?"

She thought it over before answering. "Truth be told, I can't think of any flaws at the moment. The main character, Howard Knightly, is everything you want in a hero: brave, victorious, a gentleman. The prose is smooth, and the description transports you. The only thing I would like to see in the stories isn't a flaw, per se, but rather a personal preference."

"Oh? And what's that?"

"Well, Howard is a lone adventurer, and I suppose that frees him to do all that he does. However, I can't help but wonder if he ever gets lonely."

"You think he needs a companion?" His eyebrows rose toward the brim of his straw hat.

"I think it would add even more excitement to the story if he had someone he wanted to return safely to. Someone he could, perhaps, race to save at some point. Someone who waits every time with the same bated breath as me to see if he makes it through unharmed."

"So not simply a companion but a lover."

She shrugged. "Why not both? That would be my one recommendation to the author, but I hope you don't let that spoil your view of the series. You should read it in full, just the same."

He rubbed his thumb over his bottom lip, obscuring a smile that made her nervous. Why did she feel like he was playing with her? Suddenly she wished she hadn't chosen to seclude herself from the rest of the picnic. Her gaze darted beyond the man in search of anyone that might notice her location.

"Thank you for your wonderful critique, miss. I suppose I'm past due to introduce myself." He held out his tanned hand. "August Cates, ma'am. I'm pleased to make your acquaintance."

Evelyn's mouth dropped open before she could stop the unladylike expression that would ruffle her stepmother like an irate peacock. She stared at his outstretched hand without moving.

"August Cates..." Her gaze trailed to the cover of the book where the same name was inscribed. "Not *the* August Cates."

"I'm sorry for not introducing myself sooner, but I wanted an honest review." He dropped his hand to his side. "I'm afraid critics in the magazines and readers who know my identity are biased."

"I didn't realize... I mean... I wondered who would be asking such questions." She sputtered for words. "I'm sorry if my thoughts sounded idiotic, but I really do love your books."

He placed his hand over his heart and bowed his head. "Thank you, madam. Could I have the honor of learning your name?"

"Oh, yes, I'm sorry. Evelyn Macaree." She hesitated before holding out her hand, and this time he gave it a polite shake. "If you don't mind me asking, why are you here? In Boston? At our church picnic?"

He gestured across the park at a small group of young couples playing croquet. "My brother and his new wife live here and attend church with your lovely congregation. They invited me to stay with them while I'm on a respite of sorts. I found it more appealing than my parents' stuffy home in New York where my mother would do nothing but lecture me on the straightness of my posture and my father would grumble about the lack of security in my career choice."

As he spoke, Evelyn sat in awe of how smoothly his words flowed from his lips. It was like listening to his prose come to life. She needed no proof that this was August Cates standing before her, but she still couldn't quite believe it.

"If you need a respite, I hope all is well."

"While trying to finish the book you hold in your hands, I fell sick in Ireland. I'm well now, and obviously, I managed to finish the book. I still felt I was overdue for a vacation." He sunk to sit against the tree, propping his arm on his raised knee.

"Ireland?" She straightened her spine. "Have you seen the Cliffs of Moher yourself?"

His mysterious grin returned. It was exactly how she imagined Howard Knightly's grin—somehow both audacious and charming. "I've stood on the edge of the Cliffs of Moher."

"And this flying machine? I've seen pictures of the Wrights' invention, but have you flown one yourself?"

"I wish, but no. Did you hear about Wilbur Wright's demonstrations in France two years ago?"

"Yes, I read about it in the paper."

"I watched him complete figure eights with my own eyes. As soon as airplanes become passenger-ready, I'm going to experience flight for myself."

She sucked in a breath. "Have you been on all of Howard Knightly's adventures then?"

He nodded. "I've ridden a camel across a desert. I've climbed a pyramid. I still feel I failed to capture the remarkable view in my story. I've hiked through the dense foliage of the Amazon. One year I spent most of my time aboard a boat, sailing to many different islands, including the Hawaiian Islands. One of my favorite things has been staring an elephant in the eye. Magnificent beasts."

She ran her hand over the cover as she stared at the picture of Howard on the edge of the cliff. "No wonder I always feel like

I'm beside Howard during all of his adventures. That must be a thrilling way to live."

"I'm blessed to do what I do and live by it. It's readers like you that allow me the honor." He paused, his gaze drifting across the park. "I wish I could do more to return the favor, but all I can do is write books that you enjoy. That's why I was asking your opinion. My publishers and critics are always the ones telling me how to improve my books, but I wanted to hear the opinion of a true reader."

"I would be happy even if you never changed a thing. The adventure in foreign lands is all I need." She bit her lip as she hugged the book to her chest. "Your words take me to places I will probably never get the chance to go. Your books bring the world to me."

Her face heated as she spilled such intimate feelings, but it was the truth. She had discovered his books while adjusting to a new life with a stepmother and stepsisters who treated her with contempt. In her own world, she felt trapped, unseen, and small, but Howard Knightly always swept her far away on thrilling adventures, even if it was only for a few minutes at a time. She never realized how much she craved a life outside of the four walls of her family's home until she found it in those books.

August watched her with a mysterious expression she couldn't cipher.

"But if you do change anything"—she cleared her throat—"I think giving Howard a companion of sorts would be a lovely idea."

He nodded slowly, plucking a blade of grass to roll between his fingers. "Thank you. I'll add that to my list of ideas." He dropped the grass blade to pull a small notebook from his pants pocket along with a stubby pencil.

She watched in curiosity as he scribbled something down. "You actually have an idea list on you?"

He waved the notebook. "A writer never leaves home without a means to write."

Their eyes met again, and it made her breath catch. He flashed a contagious grin, which she couldn't help but return. Was it possible he modeled Howard Knightly after himself? Perhaps the blond-haired, blue-eyed hero looked different than the plain man in front of her, but every bit of Howard's confidence seemed to emanate from August with an easy charisma and affable openness.

"I realize you're on respite, but do you already have plans for another book?" She craned her neck to peek at his notebook.

He slid it back into his pocket. "I'm afraid that's a secret between myself and my publisher."

She blushed. "Of course. My apologies."

"Nothing is set in stone yet. That's another thing I'm hoping to solve while in Boston."

"Evelyn, where have you been?" Dahlia marched up to them, only giving August a fleeting glance. "Mother has a headache and has been ready to leave for ages."

Swallowing her disappointment, Evelyn tucked the book away in her bag. "It was lovely meeting you, Mr. Cates. How long do you plan to be in town?"

"I'm not sure, but I believe I'll see you next week in church?" He ended the sentence with a questioning tone, his eyes filling with a hopefulness that caused a curious flutter in her chest.

"Most definitely. Have a wonderful week, Mr. Cates."

As she followed Dahlia across the park to the rest of their waiting family, she wished it was the next Sunday already. She wanted to ask him so much more about his adventures and his writing.

August even managed to help her forget about Daniel, at least for a few minutes.

CHAPTER 4

$\mathcal{E}$velyn poked at her eggs. Her stepmother's chatter was a distant hum behind her thoughts. Staying up the night before until her bedside candle was gone, Evelyn had finished *Peril on the Cliffs of Moher*.

In the end, Howard Knightly once again successfully thwarted Dr. Draper's disastrous plans. At the climax of the heart-stopping action sequence, Dr. Draper's flying machine chased Howard to the treacherous edges of the Cliffs of Moher. The fiend left Howard with no way out, but full of courage, Howard did the least expected thing: he stepped off the cliffs of his own free will.

His daring decision saved his life, preventing Dr. Draper from sweeping him off into the churning seas below, and instead, Howard was able to safely fall to a ledge where Dr. Draper's flying machine couldn't reach him. Evelyn had found herself powerless to do anything but turn the pages as Howard used rocks from his safe ledge to disable the flying machine, sending it and the doctor into the angry waves.

After putting the book down, her dreams were full of flying

machines and daring cliff adventures. Even fully awake she wanted to keep living in that fantastical world.

Except August Cates told her that world wasn't merely fictional. It was a real place, though far away. What would it feel like to stand on the edge of those cliffs, the salty sea breeze blowing her dark curls into hopeless tangles? The only sound for miles would be the gulls circling in the sky and water crashing against the rocks below.

What would it be like to see it? The thought nearly stole her breath, and she nibbled on a bite of eggs as she continued to mull the idea. She had never left Boston, let alone the country. Of course, she had heard of the rich taking tours of Europe for vacation, but she never considered the idea. Where would she get the funds? Or the chaperone? Her father wouldn't let her go alone as an unmarried woman.

"Evelyn!"

Her fork clattered to her plate as she jumped. Coming out of her daydream, she found her stepmother glaring at her.

"Why does it seem your head is in the clouds more than it's out of it?" Prudence pressed her lips together, shooting her husband a knowing look.

Evelyn's gaze flickered between them, but her father continued to eat his food, absorbed in the newspaper resting beside his plate.

"I'm sorry. I was just... Did I miss something?" Evelyn asked.

Prudence rolled her eyes and shook her head. "You do realize, Edwin, that this comes as a result of those novels you indulge her with. What good does fantasy do for a person? A young woman should focus on more important things, like learning how to keep the house so she has some chance at finding a decent husband."

Evelyn closed her eyes, bracing herself against her stepmother's tirade.

Father cleared his throat, placing his napkin by his plate. "I don't want to be late for work. I'll see you all this evening."

He rose, and as he passed around the table, he paused behind Evelyn. She straightened in surprise when he stooped to peck her on the cheek. How long had it been since he bid her farewell before going to work?

"Don't tax your stepmother," he whispered in her ear before straightening.

She wilted at his words. A moment later, the slam of the front door announced his exit.

"Don't forget today is rug day." Prudence stood, toast crumbs cascading off her satin skirt. "However, your sisters and I need to call on Mrs. Wimple. It's only been a week since her husband passed, and we need to make sure she's managing. So you'll have to stay and help Lottie."

"Yes, ma'am. Please give Mrs. Wimple my regards."

Prudence strode from the room, and her daughters followed like little ducklings in matching linen day dresses.

After Evelyn helped Lottie with the breakfast dishes, they dragged the large oriental rug from the sitting room out to the laundry lines. Lottie used the woven wood carpet beater to pelt the dirt from the rug, and Evelyn joined in with the broom. They worked in silence with narrowed eyes and held breaths as dust billowed out of the carpet fibers.

When they paused to rest their arms and let the dust settle, Lottie glanced at Evelyn. "I hope your stepmother's words at breakfast haven't got you down."

"They weren't false." She kept her gaze fastened on the rug. It was always satisfying to see a noticeable difference. "I daydream more than I ought to."

"You've always been a dreamer, and your father finds it endearing. Or at least he used it. Said your mother encouraged it in you." Lottie wiped her brow on her sleeve before lifting the carpet beater again.

Evelyn pressed her lips together as they began beating the rug on the other side. It was true that her mother encouraged it. She'd introduced Evelyn to novels at a young age and incited her to spin stories of her own whenever they did housework together. It fostered in Evelyn a love of caring for their home and letting her mind wander to distant realms at the same time. Maybe it was endearing for a child to dream and chase fantasies, but she had grown since her mother's passing.

She paused the broom to gaze at the back of their modest home that sat sandwiched between other townhouses of mirror size. The greenery snaking up the lattice to the attic window lived on in memory of her mother's care. Family was all that Mother needed. All that she lived for, crediting the Lord for that blessing. That's what Evelyn wanted, but most days it seemed her imagination wouldn't leave her alone.

Could she have both if she were to marry someone like Daniel? The thought struck her like a lightning bolt, causing her to freeze with the broom on the rug.

By his rich, powerful side, things like vacations in Europe were a possibility, and she could start the family of her dreams, filling her own home with the same love and care she learned from her mother.

Evelyn tried to shake the thought as they moved onto the next rug from the house. Marrying Daniel was as fanciful as any other dream of adventure, but even while she tried to focus on the chore at hand, a longing filled her chest for the possibilities unraveling in her mind.

Once the downstairs rugs had all been thoroughly beaten, Lottie declared a lunch break, and Evelyn gratefully lowered the broom from her weary arms. Since her stepfamily was nowhere to be found, the two women took their lunch at the island barstools in the center of the kitchen.

Evelyn chewed her cold meat sandwich as she watched light filter through the kitchen window. Try as she might, she couldn't keep her mind focused on the rugs they still had left to clean. Instead, it frolicked through the ideas of Irish cliffs and the rush of flying machines.

"You've worked hard this morning, miss," Lottie commented as she carried her plate to the sink. "Let's take half an hour more rest. That'll give me time to do these dishes."

"I can help with the dishes," Evelyn offered.

Lottie shooed her away as she slipped her plate into the sink. "I'm the one paid for the work. Go rest yourself."

Evelyn gave her housekeeper's shoulders a grateful squeeze before leaving the kitchen. Carried by her daydreams, Evelyn went up the two flights of stairs to her attic bedroom. Her trunk of books waited with eye-catching covers and the intoxicating aroma of paper and ink, beckoning her to crack open a spine and disappear for her half hour of break. She ran her finger over the spines of her beloved books.

She never tired of reading the Howard Knightly books, but her spirit stirred for a new adventure. Something she hadn't experienced before. Her gaze drifted to the small desk in the corner of the room as a new idea came to her. She sat at the desk and pulled an unused leather journal from one of the drawers. After sharpening the tip of her pencil with a small pen knife, she poised it over the clean piece of paper.

"Evie, tell me a story to make the work pass by. What adventure are we going on today?" Her mother's warm voice filled her memory. Evelyn rested the pencil tip on the paper, trying to piece together the image of the adventure her heart yearned for.

A heroine materialized in her mind, full of courage and grace. Ready to face whatever befell her as she faced the world. An unforgettable smile filled Evelyn's chest with an equal measure of ache and warmth.

Feeling as if her mother watched over her shoulder, she wrote the first words that came to mind.

These are the adventures of Rose Wheelock, who dared to live each day like it was her last.

~

"SHE IS IMPROVING, ISN'T SHE?" PRUDENCE BEAMED AT FLORENCE on the piano.

Evelyn glanced at Dahlia, who feigned focus on her embroidery, but Evelyn didn't miss the short look she shot her twin sister.

Florence stuck her tongue at Dahlia while their mother thumbed through pages of music, unaware. Evelyn bit her lip to hide a smile as she focused on mending Prudence's skirt. Her knees ached from kneeling in one place for so long, but the hole was nearly closed. She admired her handiwork with a hint of pride. The rip would barely be noticeable by the time she finished. Maybe her sewing was improving.

"Play this one next." Prudence leaned over to set the music in front of Florence.

Evelyn paused her needle until Prudence stilled again, but she couldn't stop a cringe as Florence began the new song with gusto. Was this song even supposed to be played with such force?

The knocker on the front door made everyone in the sitting room pause, but no one moved to answer it even when the caller knocked again.

"I'll answer that." Evelyn set aside her sewing, grateful for the excuse to stretch her legs.

She hurried into the front hall after brushing a few thread clippings from her black skirt. She swept the front door open and froze at the sight of the gentleman on the front step.

Daniel Prindall removed his flat-brimmed hat, bending his head in an almost bow. "Ms. Macaree, I believe?"

Evelyn stared, her mouth parting but no words coming out.

"Evelyn, who's at the door?" Prudence stepped into the hall.

Evelyn gripped the doorknob as she tried to push back the panic clawing at her chest. "Mr. Prindall, will you please come in?"

"Thank you, miss." He stepped inside, handing over his hat at her offered hand. "Mrs. Macaree, I presume. I apologize for dropping by unannounced." As he respectfully nodded to Prudence, his tall build seemed to fill their entry hall. A confident air demanding respect and attention radiated off his straight spine and broad shoulders, but a shy kindness overshadowed his regal posture as he smiled at Evelyn.

"Young Master Prindall." Prudence returned the nod, her countenance taking on a more formal air that failed to match his. "For what reason do we have the pleasure of your presence?"

"I came to speak to Ms. Macaree alone, if I may be so bold to request." He turned his piercing blue gaze back to her.

Evelyn's stomach flipped, and she was unable to tear her gaze from his. How had she possessed the boldness a few days ago to kiss this man in his garden? Now she could barely meet his eyes without her face heating.

"Girls, I believe we have some things upstairs to attend to," Prudence called over her shoulder into the sitting room.

"But—" Florence rose from the piano bench.

"Come." Prudence motioned to the stairs.

She waited for her daughters to hurry upstairs and then followed, but Evelyn didn't miss the glance Prudence shot over her shoulder before disappearing out of sight.

"Please, have a seat." Evelyn motioned into the sitting room. Her throat threatened to close and cut off all air supply, but she forced herself to maintain normal breathing patterns. The presence of one man should not have the ability to wreck her entire system.

Why on earth had he come? Surely Edith hadn't told him the

truth after promising not to. Was he there to tell her to never make an appearance before him again? To shame her for crashing his nice party and deceiving him into thinking she was one of them?

Daniel sat on the edge of a straight-backed chair, but he waited for Evelyn to sit in the chair next to him before speaking, his knee beginning to bounce. "I wanted to return something that I believe belongs to you."

"Me?" Evelyn squeaked out the word.

Daniel reached into his pocket, and as he retracted his hand, a small chain dangled into view, a familiar cross hanging from the end. She sucked in a breath as relief flooded through her at the sight of her mother's necklace.

"So it is yours." He raised his sandy eyebrows.

"How did you know? How did you find it?" She held out her cupped hand, and he dropped the necklace on her palm.

"I found it in the garden after you left. It appeared the clasp was loose." He smiled as he leaned back in the chair. "It helped me find you again."

"Thank you for returning it," she murmured.

"I hope you don't mind that I replaced the loose clasp. Hopefully, it won't lose its owner ever again."

She gripped the necklace in her fist against her stomach. "Thank you. I can repay you for that."

"It's the least I could do to thank you."

"Thank me? What for?"

"For the most wonderful evening I've ever had at a party."

Shock shot up Evelyn's spine. He wasn't there to tell her off. "I still don't... how did you..."

"Edith told me," he admitted. "But please don't get mad at her for it. I forced it out of her. I had a feeling the mysterious lady from the party dropped that necklace, and Edith's eyes nearly bugged out of her head when I showed her. You have to understand. I couldn't let her go without telling me, and as her brother, I have my ways of extracting information." His boyish smile caused twin dimples to emerge.

Was it possible for his clean-cut, symmetrical face to look any more handsome?

Evelyn cleared her throat, trying to hide the effect of his smile by focusing on toying with the necklace. "I hope she didn't go through too much torture hiding my secret."

"I threatened to hold her down for Daisy until she told, but she relented before one lick could be made." He laughed. "Daisy is my—"

"Dog, yes," Evelyn finished for him. "I remember her."

His eyebrows scrunched before recognition lit his eyes. "That's right. You've been friends with my sister for many years, haven't you? I can't believe I didn't recognize you sooner. I suppose I never realized the gem of a friend my sister had."

Evelyn ducked her head, hoping he didn't notice the blush spreading from her cheeks to her ears. A rustle in the hall drew her attention to the doorway, and she caught sight of a tuft of fabric peeking around the corner. So much for her stepfamily having something to attend upstairs. Her blush burned hotter.

Daniel cleared his throat. "I'm sorry if my words made you uncomfortable. I probably sound rather strange to you, but I haven't been able to get Saturday's party—or you—out of my mind. Your wit. Your kindness."

She raised her gaze to search for sincerity in his face. Was she hearing his words correctly? He thought of her as witty that night? She remembered no wit, just freely being herself for once in her life. No timidity holding her back.

"You don't have to apologize," she murmured. "That night was magical and memorable for me as well. I'm sorry if you took my shocked silence the wrong way. I never imagined you would feel the same way, so all of this is taking me by surprise."

"Truthfully?" The hopefulness in his expression brought a warmth to her chest that melted some of her discomfort.

She nodded. "I'm sorry I didn't reveal my identity to you then. I feared you would be disappointed if you knew I'm the daughter of one of your factory managers."

"And? You held your own against all of us moguls just fine." He stood from the chair, fiddling with the gold cuff link on his left wrist. "I won't take up more of your time since I dropped by unexpectedly. I've probably shocked you enough for one visit."

"Thank you again for fixing my necklace."

"My pleasure." He hesitated, his gaze seeming to search her face. "Would you allow me the honor of calling on you again? Perhaps as soon as tomorrow evening? I realize your father is at work now, but I'll come after dinnertime so that I can meet him as well as the rest of your family."

She willed herself to gather some of her past courage as she met his eyes. "I'd like that."

"We can go on a walk," he suggested as he stepped toward the door.

"That would be nice." She stood to see him out.

She took his hat off the rack by the door to offer it to him. He placed his hand on the brim, their fingers brushing, but he made no move to take it from her.

"I'd like to get to know Evelyn Macaree as more than just the mysterious woman at that party," he murmured, his breath close enough to tickle her hair.

Their kiss flashed through her memory, but she willed herself not to grow shy again. "I'd like to get to know you as well."

"Until then." He finally took his hat before stepping out the door.

She watched him walk down their front steps, his slender frame perfectly showcased in his light-colored suit—a suit probably worth more than her entire wardrobe.

After closing the front door, she leaned against it to catch her breath.

Daniel Prindall had been in her house. Daniel Prindall found their evening as enchanting as she had. Daniel Prindall was going to call on her again.

Had she finally daydreamed herself right into a fantasy world?

CHAPTER 5

*E*velyn sneaked a glance at Daniel. He walked straight and tall beside her with his hands clasped behind his back. He looked every bit the casual gentleman in his ivory linen suit and straw hat with a wide navy band. She felt like a small work rag next to him in her purple cotton dress, which lacked any decoration, but she had thought to add a sash around the waist to draw a little more shape out of it. Even though the unusually warm spring evening didn't require it, she also draped a creamy white shawl around her shoulders.

Why, at a moment like this, was she nitpicking their outfits of all things? Why wasn't she engaging him in some sort of witty discussion instead of walking with her tongue glued to the roof of her mouth?

She stifled a sigh. Perhaps it was because, in all her daydreaming, she never imagined she would get to this point, yet here she was. Not only had Daniel returned that evening to see her, but he also spoke to her father as promised. Of course, her father would never refuse his boss's son anything, including permission to court his daughter.

They strode together down the Boston sidewalk, the town

around them bathed in orange light from the sunset. The man of her dreams walked next to her. What came next?

She glanced at him again and started to speak at the same time he did.

They both paused, their gazes meeting. She blushed as he smiled with one corner of his mouth.

"Ladies first." He motioned to her.

"I was going to say thank you for inviting me on this walk." She drew her shawl a little tighter for security rather than warmth. "It's a beautiful evening."

"The evening is not the only beautiful thing."

Her heart tripped, and she had to concentrate on the placement of her feet to keep from stumbling.

He cleared his throat before letting out a choked laugh. "I apologize if that was too bold." Red crept up his neck around the collar of his shirt. Maybe she wasn't the only one nervous. "My mother tried to teach me how to be a proper gentleman, but I'm afraid that was one of the lessons I only half-listened to."

"Oh." She wanted to smack herself the second it left her lips. Oh? That was the most intelligent reply she could come up with? How about, "On the contrary, I've never met a more perfect gentleman"? She should meet his boldness toe to toe.

She cleared her throat, deciding on a safer approach. "Edith tells me that you work with your father, overseeing his factories. Do you enjoy it?"

"Yes, quite. I've known since I was young that I would follow in my father's footsteps, and my college education was centered on business management. I rushed through it so I could get to the interesting part of actually running the business."

"Even if you rushed, you must have excelled in your studies to be top of your class."

She bit the inside of her cheek as his eyebrows shot up.

"Just how much do you and my sister talk about me?" His smile widened with his teasing tone.

She toyed with the fringe of her shawl as she looked at a bakery they passed. "She mentioned you on occasion. She was proud of you."

"Hm. I suppose it was bold of me again to hope that you were the one asking about me."

As he focused ahead, she dared to study his face. How much had Edith told him about her past infatuation with him? She would die and perhaps kill Edith if she had breathed a word of her childish, longstanding feelings.

"I feel a bit at a disadvantage here," he admitted. "My sister has told you about me, but I know next to nothing about you."

Perhaps Edith was safe for the time being. "There's not much to know, I'm afraid, but you can ask anything."

"Has your family always lived in Boston?"

"Before I was born, at least. As far as I know, my parents both lived here their entire lives as well."

"But your mother is not the Mrs. Macaree I've met. That much I know from Edith."

"My mother is, or I suppose was, Rose Macaree. We lost her when I was eight years old, but she taught me all I know about family, love, and faith." A warm peace seemed to seep from her core as she talked about her mother, drawing the tension out of her shoulders.

"She sounds like a wonderful woman," he murmured. "And she must have been to raise such a wonderful daughter."

"She was the best."

"One thing I'm curious about is how you met my sister. Did you go to school together?"

"No. After my mother passed away, I didn't enjoy going to our silent house after school. I preferred joining my father at his factory and reading in his office while I waited for him to complete his work. I don't remember why, but one day Edith joined your father on a tour of his factories. While our fathers discussed business, the two of us became fast friends. Edith has such an inviting personality. I'm beginning to wonder if it's a Prindall characteristic."

To her surprise, Daniel laughed. "I'd like to think all of us Prindalls possess what Edith has, but she has her own special way of drawing people in. She could befriend a recluse."

When she laughed with him, the rest of her discomfort seemed to dissipate. Even though his formal appearance was a bit intimidating, there was still something warm about his presence. Something that made her think she could trust his intentions.

As they continued their walk without any specific destination, she asked more about his schooling, and he in turn asked more about her family, which she answered with some vagueness to avoid the conversation looping back to her stepfamily in a way that would force her to divulge too much. When they circled back toward her house, her heart sank in disappointment. It felt like the walk had passed in a matter of seconds.

"Thank you for accompanying me this evening." He took her hand to help her up the stoop.

She ignored the movement of the curtains over the front window as she focused on him. "Thank you for asking me. I thoroughly enjoyed it."

"Perhaps I could have the honor of visiting you again soon?" The hope in his voice melted her heart into the bottom of her shoes. "If your father agrees, of course."

"I would like that." She let them into the house.

In an instant, her stepmother and father joined them in the entry to ask how their walk was, and Evelyn spied her stepsisters peeking out of the sitting room. After asking her father for permission to call again, which he granted without hesitation, Daniel excused himself for the evening.

Before leaving, he bent over her hand to brush her knuckles with a kiss. As he did, his sharp blue eyes rose to meet hers, and she found herself captivated by the intense expression in them.

He truly was interested in her. Had the Lord heard the prayers of her heart?

As if an answer to her doubts, Daniel called on her again almost every evening for the rest of the week. Whether it was dinner at a nice restaurant or simply relaxing in her family's sitting room, Evelyn soaked in every moment with him. There was something unbelievable about a man of his station sitting in her tiny house, entertaining a girl like her, but across from him, she could forget her stepmother who still spoke harshly every day. She could ignore her stepsisters who treated her like muck on the bottom of their shoes.

Her friendship with Edith kept her from feeling entirely unloved in the years since her mother's passing, but the way Daniel looked at her made her feel different than ever before. Was this the beginning of the love she had prayed would sweep her far away from the pains of her current life? It sure seemed like it, but every time she met his boyish smile, something deep in her mind wondered when she would wake from this dream.

When she lay in bed at night, reliving every sweet moment with Daniel, something whispered that he might grow tired of her. It whispered doubts about whether he would ever want to marry her. What dowry did she have to offer? Men of his station married for advantage and title. She had neither. Would his interest last?

Friday evening, he invited her to an opera with his family, and for one evening she was able to step back into the fairytale feelings she experienced at the party. Once again, Edith lent her a dress and did her makeup and hair. From the moment she followed Edith down the Prindall's grand front staircase after getting around for the evening, Daniel didn't take his eyes off her. His sweet whispers meant for her ears only on the automobile ride over to the theater made her stomach dance with pleasure. Maybe he truly did care.

She tried to keep her head high as the evening progressed in a whirlwind upon their arrival at the theater. Daniel introduced her to friends from his college days, work colleagues of his father, and many people who could be considered the royalty of Boston. Evelyn struggled to remember every etiquette lesson Prudence had barked at her. How did she know when to offer her hand and what greeting to apply?

When they finally reached their seats, her shoulders were stiff with anxiety, but Daniel's gentle squeeze to her hand undid it all in an instant. She glanced up into his clear blue eyes and let herself breathe.

The performers flitted across the stage, belting in a language she couldn't understand, but her attention remained fastened on the hand in hers. It felt impossible that a week ago he didn't even know her name, but now they sat together in his family's private box, making all the social elites whisper about their relationship.

In the darkness of the theater, her gaze traced the outline of his handsome features, and despite the anxieties still knotting her stomach, her heart whispered a prayer to the Lord.

Thank You for taking the loneliness away.

CHAPTER 6

*E*velyn stepped out of her family's home with her journal clamped between her teeth, still trying to pin her straw hat over her bun. Her eyes caught the backside of the hired carriage that carried her father down the street. Removing the journal from her mouth, she hugged it to her chest as she watched the carriage until it turned the corner. He had claimed it was an urgent matter relating to a supplier that carried him away from his family on the one day set aside for rest, but how urgent could the matter be that it couldn't wait until Monday?

Determined to shake off the hurt, she turned her face toward the bright spring sun. It had quickly burned away the overcast morning, and a warm breeze chased off any remaining chill. Evelyn let the fresh air fill her lungs and carry her down the steps to the street.

Any day as beautiful as this deserved to be enjoyed, and since her father had left for work, and Daniel wouldn't be calling, she had nothing to keep her within the same confines as her step-family. Of course, even though she offered to allow them to accompany her, none of them wanted to spoil their porcelain skin with unnecessary sun exposure. So she had left the house before anyone could change their mind, closing the door on her stepmother's protests that it was improper for her to go out alone.

Evelyn navigated the few blocks between their house and the park, letting her arms swing free by her side with her journal in hand. The park seemed like the perfect place to pick up where she had left off in her story. Every spare moment she had between her stepfamily's demands and Daniel's visits, she continued to fill the pages of the journal.

She strolled into the park that was alive with activity. Couples and families scattered throughout the bright green oasis in the middle of the bustling city, taking up the available benches and picnic tables. Evelyn followed along the gravel path, letting her mind wander back to the church picnic a week ago. Had it only been a week ago?

Daniel's attentions had swept her into another time and dimension over the week since, warping her grasp on reality. Was she becoming one of those lovesick women she and Edith used to laugh at?

Now the park caused memories to resurface of her brief encounter with August Cates at the picnic, and she realized she couldn't even remember if the author had attended church that morning with his brother and sister-in-law. Daniel had been consuming her thoughts and focus, even when he wasn't at her side.

Trying to push away the creeping shame for her lovesick behavior with more memories of the picnic, Evelyn abandoned the path to approach the pond in the center of the park, and as she rounded some reeds that stood between her and the pond, her thoughts about the author seemed to materialize before her in the form of August stretched out on a picnic blanket. She stopped in her tracks as she blinked to confirm that it wasn't her imagination, but no matter how many times she blinked, he lay on his side, a book opened in front of him.

His eyes skimmed the page as he nibbled on a piece of chicken.

"Good afternoon, Mr. Cates," Evelyn said, announcing her presence.

He looked up from his book in surprise, but it melted into a warm smile. "Good afternoon, Ms. Macaree. Care to join me?" He sat up and moved his book before motioning for her to sit.

She hesitated, Prudence's voice barking about propriety filtering through her head, but curiosity drove her forward to sit next to him. After arranging her skirts around her ankles, she settled her journal in her lap.

"I came to enjoy the beautiful weather, but I don't think I was the only one with that idea." She cast a gaze around the busy park.

"Great minds think alike. Would you like something to eat? My sister-in-law packed enough to feed an army." August opened the lid of his wooden picnic basket to give her a glimpse of the goodies inside.

"That's generous. Thank you, but I've already eaten."

"I'm glad I've run into you again. I feel like we didn't have enough time to talk last week." August slipped his book into the basket before closing the lid and turning his full attention to her.

"Have you been able to enjoy some rest this week?" she asked as she leaned back on her palms.

"My version of rest, at least. My brother and sister-in-law allow me to come and go as I please, and I've been filling my days with galavants across the city, exploring shops and museums. Boston has a wealth of history and interest. It's nice to take things in for pleasure for a change and not be bothered with trying to figure out how to describe what I'm seeing."

When she raised her eyebrows, he shook his head with a smile. "I sound like I'm complaining about my occupation. I'm not, mind you. A change is... nice. It's been needed." He patted the picnic basket. "And I mean it. If you get peckish, please help yourself. My sister-in-law is determined to double my size before I leave."

"How long do you plan to stay?" Evelyn couldn't resist grabbing a strawberry after August pulled out a ripe-looking one for himself.

He squinted into the dazzling sunbeams glittering off the surface of the pond as he chewed the sweet fruit. "I'm not sure yet. When the next book calls me away, I suppose I'll follow it."

"So you haven't begun working on the next one?"

"Not yet. Your suggestions last week alighted a bit of inspiration, but nothing clear has formed yet."

"It seems you've been all over the world in your adventures. Where else is there for Howard Knightly to go?"

"Plenty of places, I assure you." He flicked the top of his strawberry into the reeds, tilting his head to the side. "I've been out of the country so long that I think it might be time to find an adventure within the United States."

"Where would you go for an adventure here?"

"This country is so vast that the possibilities are limitless. There are swamps in Louisiana. The Rockies out west. I've heard those mountains make our eastern mountain range look like hills. Can you imagine climbing a mountain that reaches for the sky?" He paused, his eyes dazing out as if he was already traveling there in his mind. "I've only been to the Pacific Ocean once. Life on that side of the country moves at a completely different pace than here. I could use a different pace. There's the Grand Canyon that way too."

"Those all sound like amazing places for a Howard Knightly adventure." She leaned forward in excitement. "I've heard of the Grand Canyon. Can you imagine the doctor chasing him on those cliffs of peril?"

He smiled a little. "Perhaps he could run into a little lass on a small ranch who lends him a helping hand in his quest, but over time it turns into something more."

"I already can't wait to read it." She clapped her hands.

"We'll see, we'll see." As he let out a rich, deep laugh, she couldn't help but smile in return. "I'm not ready to start another book. In due time."

They lapsed into silence as they continued to nibble on the fruit from the basket. Evelyn wondered if she should excuse herself so he could continue his private picnic, but he didn't seem to mind her presence as he laid back on the blanket, folding one arm behind his head. Evelyn stretched her legs out and closed her eyes as dots of sunlight filtered through the trees to warm her face. After soaking in the warmth, she peeked at August out of the corner of her eyes. He lay with his eyes closed, but he continued to eat a steady stream of grapes.

Before she could stop herself, her mind began to draw up comparisons between Daniel and August. August wore a brown suit similar to the one he wore last week—if it wasn't the same one—unlike Daniel, whom she couldn't recall wearing the same thing twice in her company. He always had on a new shade of white, cream, or gray.

Besides being plain and familiar, August's clothes hung loose on his frame, the cuffs around his ankles beginning to show the threads of wear, and his hair fluttered in the breeze without the restraint of any hair pomade, something she couldn't say for Daniel who never let a hair out of his carefully combed style.

Even their countenance was different. She tried to picture the two men standing side by side, but she couldn't imagine them in the same space. Daniel was proper, meticulous in the very way he moved. August carried his frame with a comfortable air, void of any stiff social etiquette.

As August's eyes flickered open, Evelyn snapped her gaze away. Heat flooded her cheeks, and she silently hoped August hadn't seen her staring. Why was she staring and comparing the two men?

August sat up on his elbow to rummage in the basket, and Evelyn busied herself with opening her journal to where she left off in her story. The idea of relaxing in the park and writing in her journal seemed to be the perfect way to spend the afternoon earlier, but now she had to school her thoughts into focusing on the words already on the page.

She stared at the words before allowing her gaze to wander with her thoughts. A small family picnicking across the pond caught her attention. The little girl chased a scruffy dog, stirring a memory almost forgotten. A memory of picnicking with her own parents. Romping in the grass with her father, their laughter filling the air. Her mother's sweet smile from where she sat in the shade, watching them.

When her father had declared an intermission in their game, flopping in the grass as he gasped for breath, Evelyn had settled down with her head in her mother's lap. As her mother's delicate fingers stroked through her curls, she started spinning a new story about a girl who found a hidden world full of fairies and other mythical beasts in a garden. Her father had asked about each character and creature, lightheartedly nitpicking that the fairies should have magic, but the rabbits couldn't.

Evelyn picked up her pencil as the memory stirred something in her spirit. She let the faraway images of her memory transition to faint glimpses of her current story, and her pencil scratched at the paper to capture what she saw in her mind's eye. After several minutes of writing, she became aware of August's steady gaze on her. She glanced his way, another blush burning her cheeks.

"What are you writing?" he asked.

"Oh. Well." Evelyn tightened her grip on her journal. "A story."

He raised one eyebrow in a silent question.

She licked her lips, her mind racing to figure out how to sum it up. "It's a story." She closed her eyes at her redundancy. Her story seemed like addlebrained mush compared to his books. "About a woman named Rose Wheelock who lives a daring life. Truthfully, I'm still figuring it out. I started it on a simple idea, and I keep adding a little more each day."

"May I read it?" August pushed himself upright.

Her eyes widened, and the stricken panic must have shown on her face because he laughed, holding up a hand.

"If you aren't comfortable with that, you don't need to feel obligated to show me. I understand the sacredness of a story in the beginning stages of creation."

She stared down at the writing on the page, nibbling on the edge of her lip. "I haven't let anyone read it yet. Until you, I hadn't even told anyone I'm writing a story."

"What prompted you to start it?"

"My mother. At least in a way. When I was younger, my mother encouraged me to come up with stories. I always had an endless imagination, and I suppose she enjoyed listening to my fanciful daydreams." She ran her hand over the page. "Actually, you're to blame as well. Your wonderful works inspired me to chase an adventure of my own, and my imagination is the only way to do that at the moment. I doubt I could ever publish it though."

"Keep writing." He drew up his knees and rested his arms on them. "Even if you don't show another living soul. The author needs their story as much as anyone else."

Evelyn flipped through the pages until she reached the first sentence that began her little journey. The only person she wanted to share this story with was her mother. As she stared at the words on the page, the temptation of August's request niggled at her mind. What if, someday, she did want to share her writing with others? Writing this story had been more enjoyable than she imagined. She could see it becoming an addicting pastime. If she ever wanted a fair assessment of her writing abilities, wouldn't a published author be a good second option? But if it was terrible and he told her so, what would she do?

Keep the story to herself as she was already doing.

Before she could second guess herself any longer, she held the journal out toward August. "Perhaps you could offer a decent opinion on the beginning. As I said, I don't plan to do anything with it, but now I'm curious to see if it's worth anything at all."

"I'd be honored." The warmth in his voice as he took the journal told her he meant it.

She couldn't look at him as he read the story in silence. She stared at the pond while nibbling on her thumbnail. An eternity seemed to pass, with only the sound of the turning pages between them.

When August closed the journal, her gaze flew to his face to try to find any hint of his thoughts.

"You're an avid reader, and it shows in the beauty of your prose." He smiled as he handed the journal back to her.

"So it wasn't nonsensical garbage?" She hugged the journal to her chest.

He laughed with a shake of his head. "Far from it. Rose is an interesting character. I was so caught up in her story that it was jarring to reach the end of what you've written. I wanted to keep going."

"Truthfully?" She breathed the word, unable to believe what she was hearing.

"As I said, keep writing. Your mother's encouragement might have birthed the next great novelist. I love her already, and I haven't even met her."

Evelyn's gaze dropped to her lap, and she toyed with the ribbon hanging from the bottom of the journal. "She passed away when I was eight, but writing this story makes me feel close to her again."

"I'm so sorry for your loss," August whispered. "What was she like?"

Evelyn closed her eyes, and for a moment, she could see her mother's smiling face in her memory. "Like Rose Wheelock. Beautiful. Joyful. Lived every day like it was her last. She taught me everything I know about love and faith. I realized when she was gone that she was the spirit of our family, and after she passed away, things were never the same again. It was like the life was sucked out of our family."

Evelyn stilled when she realized how much she was pouring out to this man she had only met a week ago, but when she glanced at him, the open expression he watched her with washed away the awkward feelings. The depth of emotion in his eyes almost made her believe that he could empathize.

"I'm sorry for rambling." Evelyn tucked a loose curl behind her ear. "I'm sure you've heard enough about me to last a lifetime."

"Don't apologize. You've listened to me rattle on about my writing and travels enough. I wanted to hear about you for a change." He hesitated, his brows lowering with a thoughtful expression. "You attend church with what I assumed is your family. Does that mean your father remarried?"

"Yes, and now I have twin stepsisters as well."

She pressed her hands into her skirt, trying to think of a polite way to excuse herself without revealing to him that his questions about her stepfamily made her uncomfortable. She already revealed more than she should have about her life, and the troubles of her stepfamily were not something else she wanted to divulge.

"Speaking of my family, I should return home before they worry." She started to push herself to her feet when August's hand shot out and caught the lace cuff of her blouse.

She froze with wide eyes, but his attention was trained on her wrist. She followed his gaze to the four distinct bruises the shape of Prudence's fingertips. His eyes raised to hers with a question in their dark depths.

She turned her face away as she stood, tugging her sleeve lower. "I really should go."

A sick feeling settled in her gut at the memory of Prudence's rage after she returned from the opera with Daniel. Her fanciful night was shattered by Prudence's accusation that she had chipped one of their china plates. When she denied the accusation, Prudence had shaken her until all the hairpins rattled out of her hair, undoing Edith's hard work. Prudence didn't relent in her accusations until Evelyn's father came to investigate the shouting.

Evelyn couldn't even remember chipping the china the last time she helped Lottie dust the cabinet, but Prudence was convinced Evelyn deliberately sabotaged the beautiful gift from her wedding to Evelyn's father.

"Do they hurt you?" August whispered.

"Goodbye, Mr. Cates." She turned on her heels to flee.

"Ms. Macaree—" He cut himself off. "I'm sorry."

"You have nothing to apologize for." She stood still, her shoulders stiff.

"For crossing boundaries I shouldn't have. We haven't known each other long, and I shouldn't have touched you. But no one deserves to be hurt by those who are supposed to love them."

She swallowed, glancing over her shoulder. His concern reminded her of Edith. How many others simply looked past the marks and bruises inflicted by her stepmother? Even Lottie. Even herself. "Thank you for your concern, but it isn't as bad as I'm sure you're imagining. I'm all right." The words sounded flat to her own ears, but she forced a smile to accompany them.

He stuffed his hands in his pockets, his lips pressed in a line. "Why don't you leave?"

She frowned. "What do you mean?"

"Why do you stay with them if they treat you badly?"

She helplessly held up a hand. "What other choice do I have? Someday I want to marry and start a family of my own, but until then, what else can I do?" Her mind drifted to the past week with Daniel, and she dared to let her heart lift at the idea of the escape he may one day provide her.

"This is the twentieth century." August spread his arms out. "You could get a job of your own. There are plenty of respectable jobs fit for single women, and there are whole apartment buildings and houses dedicated to providing safe, respectable living to women. My sister-in-law lived in one, working as a secretary before she married my brother. I can ask her for recommendations on jobs and living spaces if you need me to."

She took a step back as the suggestion took her by surprise. Live on her own? She wasn't naive to the idea that women were finding more independence than ever before in the new century, but the concept was foreign in her world. The very thought repulsed her. She didn't want that. She wanted a house full of love.

"Thank you for your concern, but I really am all right."

The worry in his eyes didn't lessen. "My offer still stands, should you ever need it."

"Thank you. Have a good day, Mr. Cates."

"It's August, please."

She hesitated before nodding. "All right. Have a good day, August."

She turned on her heels and walked away before he could say anything else to draw her back in. She started toward the gravel path, but she found herself glancing over her shoulder at August again. He stood with his hands stuffed deep into his pockets, his gaze fastened on the pond.

She didn't know how to feel about him as she continued on the same path that brought her into the park. He seemed genuine and kind, but he also seemed to view things from a perspective she had never experienced before. Everything about him was different than what she was accustomed to. He was almost...exotic. In fashion. In manners. In ideas.

As she held her journal to her chest, her mind returned to his encouragement about her writing. She would keep writing, and she wanted him to read whatever she wrote next to see what else he had to say. But would he give her more suggestions about leaving home?

When she arrived at the steps that led up to her family's front door, she gazed at the navy door adorned with a gold knocker. This was the only home she had ever known. Of course, she didn't plan to live there forever, but what if she did strike out on her own?

The idea was almost laughable in its absurdity. Prudence would faint away. Her father would question her sanity.

Striking out on her own would be a daring adventure. It would be something unknown to explore, which didn't sound altogether unappealing, but it sounded lonely.

Evelyn let herself in the front door and the sound of her stepsisters' chatter from the sitting room greeted her. She bypassed the room and went unnoticed as she climbed the stairs to the attic. Being alone in an apartment would be even worse than her little attic room above the rest of her family.

When she pushed open the door to the room, her gaze landed on a bright bouquet in a glass vase on her nightstand. Flowers Daniel brought with him when he picked her up for the opera.

She crossed the room to take a deep breath of the blossoms, and once more she let her mind return to the idea of him sweeping her away someday. At the opera, despite Edith's handiwork on her appearance, she couldn't shake the feeling of being out of place, but when she remembered the feel of his steady hand in hers, she could let the hopes of her heart take flight.

Hopes stored up over years of watching him from afar. Hopes she never thought would see the light of day.

She stood with her nose to the flowers for a couple minutes more, letting her mind dwell on all of the possibilities of a future with Daniel.

CHAPTER 7

"Will a certain someone be calling tonight?" A sly tone coated Prudence's words.

Evelyn focused on slicing the pork chop on her plate. "No, he had too many meetings today."

A strange disappointment settled on her chest despite the fact she had spent almost every night that week with him. Like the first week of their courtship, he led her on a never-ending trail of social functions, and Edith kept her steady stream of loaned dresses coming. The evening before, Daniel had introduced her to her first silent film, but her focus most of the night remained on his hand holding hers in the darkness. His thumb rubbed different patterns across her glove. As the live orchestra's accompanying soundtrack swelled to a climax, he raised their intertwined fingers to gently kiss her knuckles, his eyes still focused on the screen. Such innocent, sweet kisses made her feel like she would melt right out of the velvet theater chair.

The back of Evelyn's hand tingled with the memory, but she poked at her food, attempting to bring herself back to the present. "I'm sure his family has missed his presence since he's been so busy with me. They'll forget his face if he doesn't spend time with them."

Prudence snorted. "I'm sure they're eager for their only son to marry and settle down. I wouldn't be surprised if they encouraged his frequent visits to speed the process."

Evelyn's face flamed, and she shot a glance at her father. Where had the topic of marriage come from? "We've only been seeing each other a week and a half. It's much too early for them to think about him marrying."

"Maybe it seems soon to you, but I'm sure this is something they've thought about and planned long before you stepped into the picture. I wonder how long he plans to court you before proposing." Prudence set down her silverware as her words gained speed. "Now that I think about it, this would benefit everyone. The Prindalls would be one step closer to their next heir, and think about your father." To this, Father raised his eyebrows but kept his eyes on his plate. "Evelyn, think about the favor your father will gain with Mr. Prindall if your relationship continues with Daniel. Perhaps he'll receive a promotion as part of a wedding gift. Your new connections would gain your sisters better suitors as well."

Evelyn chewed her bite carefully in an attempt not to choke. How long had Prudence been thinking about them marrying? Not that the thought hadn't crossed her mind a million times over, but it was always a distant possibility, something to worry about after they had spent more time getting to know each other.

"Prudence, please stop talking about marriage. Daniel and I haven't even discussed it."

Prudence waved her hand in a dismissive manner. "There's no harm in planning for the future. Whenever that may be."

The mysterious tone in her voice made Evelyn look at her father again. Why wouldn't he look up from his plate? Why wouldn't he say anything in response to his wife's outrageous ideas?

Since Daniel was traditional and the perfect gentleman, she could rest assured he wouldn't propose without asking her father's permission first, but her father's stoic mask offered her no answer as to whether Daniel had approached him.

Maybe all of Prudence's words were her own hurried fantasy. A week and a half, even two weeks, was too short to be looking toward marriage, no matter how much she enjoyed Daniel's company thus far.

Just the same, perhaps she needed to talk to her father after supper. To ease her fears at least.

After everyone finished eating, Evelyn did her nightly duty of helping Lottie clean up from supper. As she washed the dishes in soapy water, her mind continued to churn Prudence's words about engagement. Maybe it was fast, but she had heard stories of such things before. A fast engagement meant a faster escape from this house.

Wasn't that what she wanted?

Once she dried the last dish and put it away, Evelyn hurried from the kitchen to find her father. Her stepfamily rested in the sitting room, but he wasn't with them. Down the hall, she found a weak beam of light shining under his closed study door.

Turning the knob as noiselessly as possible, she peeked through the small crack into the room. Her father sat at his desk, hunched over whatever ledger sat on the desktop. With a pen in hand, his focus remained fastened on his work, unaware of his ajar door.

With a sinking heart, Evelyn closed the door again. She could interrupt her father's work, but she didn't have the heart. He would probably be clipped with his words if his focus was interrupted. For now, she could reassure herself that Daniel made no hint at marriage, and neither had her father. All talk of marriage was her stepmother's grand idea.

Evelyn made her way up the two flights of stairs to her room, one hand holding the front of her skirt and the other clasped around her necklace.

Would it be such a bad thing if Daniel proposed? Maybe it felt sudden—because it was—but was that a bad thing? In their short time together, he had proven himself worthy of all her adolescent daydreams. He was kind and always seemed eager to listen to her talk. The way he opened every door, helped her in and out of her wraps, and made sure to walk between her and the street left her feeling like royalty. He may have claimed to only half-listen to his mother's etiquette lessons, but his actions spoke otherwise. She felt safe and secure by his side.

So if he did propose, what reason would she have for any answer but yes?

She paused in the doorway of her attic room, her gaze sweeping the crowded interior that barely fit her wardrobe, bed, vanity, and desk. Looking at the low, peaked ceiling, the thought of a proposal sweeping her away from her childhood home sounded a bit like paradise.

As if on cue to match her thoughts, her stepsisters' angry voices rose from the floors below. She couldn't make out more than a few words of the accusations they lobbed back and forth. Dahlia's voice drew closer as she stomped up to the second floor, followed by Florence shortly after.

"Stop following me, you cow!" Dahlia screamed.

"Girls!" Prudence's voice cut over theirs. "Do you want the neighbors to hear you going on like children?"

Evelyn closed her eyes. Didn't Prudence know the neighbors would hear her too if they could hear her daughters?

Their mother's reprimand brought their argument down a couple of octaves, but it continued beneath Evelyn's feet. She moved to the vanity to begin undoing her hair. As waves of dark curls tumbled down around her shoulders, Evelyn stared at her reflection and made up her mind. If Daniel dared to propose, she wouldn't refuse him.

A proposal from Daniel meant a life she never dreamed possible for herself. His wealth meant she would never have to do another day of housework, if she so chose. Anything she could want would be hers. She could focus solely on him and raising the sweet little family of her dreams.

CHAPTER 8

*E*velyn adjusted her brown skirt as she sat on the tufted leather seat beside Daniel. Instead of a chauffeur like they often used, Daniel drove the small automobile himself, and thanks to his windshield and canopy, she didn't need to don any ugly overcoats to protect her clothes.

Even though the trim-fit skirt and soft cream blouse were Evelyn's own, Edith had provided her a string of pearls and a large-brimmed hat covered in flowers to improve her simple attire. Daniel claimed it would be a casual walk in the park, but sitting next to him in his three-piece suit, she felt grateful for her friend's foresight.

Evelyn fiddled with the string of pearls since her cross necklace was out of reach under her blouse. The purr of the engine and rattle of the tires on the brick street drowned out any hopes of making conversation.

"Here we are," Daniel announced as he pulled the automobile to a stop along the curb. "I thought we could walk here for a bit, and then my mother is expecting us at home for dinner."

As he hopped out to come around to her door, Evelyn stared at the park before them. A cobbled path snaked through the lush green grass with gentle curves. Intermittent infant trees broke up the flat landscape, and colorful flowers circled the trees, protected by small iron fencing. Some day the trees would grow to provide shade for the wooden benches scattered throughout the park.

Daniel helped her from the automobile and led her toward the cobblestone path. "My father was a benefactor of this park."

She glanced at one of the painted benches as they passed by. "It's beautiful."

How could a park hold so much class? Maybe it was the finely dressed people who strode through it or the newness of the path and trees. Whatever it was, even the park felt a step above the one she usually visited. There was no foliage growing in the cracks of the stone path. There were no dandelions or bare spots in the grass where people chose to forge their own way. It seemed everything the Prindalls touched took on their wealth and perfection.

As they walked past a couple seated on a blanket, her mind jumped uninvited to August. His rugged, plain looks would be out of place in a park such as this. There was no tree big enough for him to lean against and scribble in his pocket notebook. There was no green pond surrounded by reeds for him to lay beside and read.

Realizing what she was doing, Evelyn chided herself for thinking about such things. This was her time with Daniel. August should be the last thing on her mind.

"Here. Over here." Daniel pulled her off the marked path to a bench a few yards into the grass.

She eased onto the bench when he motioned. From that vantage point, they could easily watch the sunset behind the three-story houses lining the park. Daniel turned to clasp her hands in his, his thumbs working over her knuckles like he often did.

"I brought you here because there's something that I want to discuss with you," he admitted, holding her gaze. "However, I want to start by apologizing if this doesn't meet your expectations."

She let out a small laugh. "My expectations? Daniel, this park is beautiful. What kind of expectations could I make about something like that?"

"No, not that." He squeezed her hands.

For the first time, she noticed the glisten of perspiration on his forehead despite the cool breeze blowing through the park. Her heartbeat changed in rhythm as his eyes darted around her face as if he didn't know where to focus.

"I don't know the proper procedures for this kind of thing," he continued. "I already told you I didn't listen much to my mother's lessons, and I didn't want to ask her because I want to do this my way. I want this to be our moment."

He released one of her hands to reach into his suit coat pocket. She stared at his arm, a surreal feeling numbing her from the inside out. What was he doing?

He slid off the bench to kneel on one knee as he pulled a black velvet box from his pocket.

"Evelyn Macaree, in the short time that I've known your name, I've come to realize what a beautiful woman I've missed all these years. I don't want to waste a moment more without you. Will you do me the honor of becoming my wife?" He opened the black box to reveal a diamond ring that twinkled in the fading sunlight.

Evelyn's eyes widened as she stared at the ring nestled in a dark velvet pillow. The silver band held one large diamond flanked by two smaller ones. Art Deco-style etchings decorated the band leading away from the diamonds.

"Evelyn?" Daniel's eyebrows drew together in concern, and she realized she was staring without saying anything.

"Daniel," she stammered. "This is so fast."

Abandoning his kneeling position, Daniel sat on the bench

next to her and cupped her cheek. "I know, but what we have doesn't need time to be proven. I mean it when I say I don't want another moment without you. Please tell me you feel the same way."

Vulnerability and hope shone in his eyes, and the heat of his fingers on her skin sunk in past her shock. Somehow she found herself nodding before she could think through the response. "Yes, I'll marry you."

A smile burst onto his face, revealing his twin dimples. "May I?" He pulled the ring from the box.

She held out her trembling hand for him to slide the ring on her finger. Had anything so expensive ever touched her skin? Before she could stare further at the exquisite ring, Daniel stood to brush a kiss onto her lips.

She closed her eyes as his soft lips on hers brought back every vivid memory from the party that began their connection, and with the memories came the swirling emotions that seemed to settle in her stomach. She allowed him to deepen the kiss a moment more before pulling back. Her mind continued to whirl, trying to process what had happened, as he sat beside her again.

He brushed a loose curl from her cheek. "Is it cliche to say you've made me the happiest man in the world?"

She tore her gaze from the diamond glittering on her finger to stare into his capturing gaze. She never wanted to stop looking at his handsome face, and soon she wouldn't have to.

"I'm so happy." The airlessness of her lungs made her words a mere wisp.

He gave her one more brief peck on the lips before standing. "I hate to rush the moment, but my parents are expecting us for dinner. I wanted to do this first so that we could surprise them."

She allowed him to pull her to her feet. "Your family doesn't know you were going to propose?"

"I wanted to surprise everyone, including you."

Her eyes widened. "Does my father know at least? Did you...?"

"Of course, I asked his permission. I would have it no other way." He tucked her hand in his elbow to lead her back to the automobile. "However, he'll be the only one not surprised tonight."

She could only nod, her tongue glued to the roof of her mouth with shock. After helping her into the front seat, Daniel went around to the other side to take his place behind the steering wheel. Evelyn turned her hand, allowing the light to catch the diamond at different angles. She hadn't seen many engagement rings, but she couldn't imagine a more beautiful one.

How can this be real? Her mind voiced the question even as her heart whispered a prayer of thanks to the Lord. Maybe Prudence knew what she was doing by bringing up the possibility of engagement so soon. It had given Evelyn a couple of days to prepare for this earth-shattering moment. Once the shock wore off, she could turn her attention to the next chapter of her life. One by Daniel's side and far away from her stepfamily.

In a few short minutes, Daniel drove through the open iron gates of his family's estate. The large limestone mansion sat far from the road, the gravel drive leading up to the sweeping front steps. Even though she had been to the estate more than once growing up, it suddenly felt different. Before, she had always visited as Edith's guest, an invisible outsider that the Prindalls never paid attention to, but now she was arriving as Daniel's fiancée, soon to be part of their family.

She stared at the many glass windows and wondered if they would live there when they married. Surely not. Daniel would likely purchase a home of their own. Even a home half the size of this one would be far larger than any home she ever imagined owning. As Daniel pulled the brakes on the automobile, she snuck one last look at her glamorous ring. This would be her new life. No more beating rugs or pruned hands from dishwater.

Her heart hammered against her ribs as Daniel helped her from the vehicle. A servant in a black suit stepped forward to take care of the vehicle, and Daniel led her up the steps to the main entrance made up of three sets of glass doors adorned by iron trim. As the butler held the center door open for them, she offered a small smile to the man she knew only as Johnson. She remembered him as the butler who used to scold her for running into the house without properly wiping her shoes after romping in the garden. Of course, Edith was equally guilty for the dirt tracked across the polished floors, but he couldn't scold "Young Mistress Edith."

They stepped into the entryway flanked with tall Grecian statues, and Daniel continued across the tile floor and the oriental rug to the main hall. If it weren't for her hand in his arm, she would have stopped at the entryway, too intimidated by the thought of making their announcement to his family.

"Daniel, are you home?" Edith's voice rang out from the stairway ahead.

A moment later, Edith's strawberry blonde curls popped over the black railing of the upper floor. As soon as she saw them, she flew down the stairs, the skirts of her white dress in hand.

"Don't let Mother see you run like that." Daniel raised his eyebrows.

"Oh shush." Edith waved her brother off as she pulled Evelyn into a hug. "Blink twice if he's driving you insane," she whispered into Evelyn's ear.

Evelyn laughed as she embraced her friend. "He would never."

Edith snorted as she pulled back. "You would be surprised by his ability to antagonize."

When Evelyn reached to take Daniel's arm again, Edith let out an ear-splitting shriek, and Evelyn stumbled in surprise as Edith snatched up her left hand.

"When did this happen?" Edith held Evelyn's hand up to catch the light of the electric chandeliers.

"A few minutes ago," Evelyn admitted. "You're the first to know."

Squealing again, Edith hopped as she hugged Evelyn. "I'm so happy for you both!"

"What is the meaning of this noise?" Mrs. Prindall's voice echoed into the entryway before she appeared out of a side hall-way. "Only someone in the process of dying would warrant that level of hysteria."

Evelyn's face burned, and she tried to untangle herself from her best friend. "I apologize, Mrs. Prindall. It's my fault Edith got so excited."

"Look what Daniel did, Mother!" Edith thrust Evelyn's hand out for Mrs. Prindall to see.

Her eyes widened in shock as Daniel grinned.

"Where is Father? I want you all to be the first to hear the news." Daniel pulled Evelyn back to his side.

She could only offer a weak smile to her speechless, soon-to-be mother-in-law.

Mrs. Prindall blinked the shock from her face and replaced it with a stiff smile. "My, my, Daniel. You took us all by surprise. I expected some sort of advanced notice."

"What Evelyn and I have is special, and I didn't want to let her slip away from me," Daniel declared, causing Evelyn to blush again.

"It seems tonight's dinner is a celebratory dinner then." A deep voice caused Evelyn to jump in surprise.

Mr. Prindall stood on the final step of the sweeping stair-case, and his gaze followed her hand and the ring. Evelyn had always recognized where Daniel got his handsome looks. Other than the graying at his temples, he looked to be a nearly mirror image of Daniel, complete with the same strong, confident posture, but the intensity of his clear blue eyes created an intimidating quiver in Evelyn's belly.

"The cook informed me shortly before you arrived that dinner was finished," Mrs. Prindall announced. "Shall we?"

Mrs. Prindall led the way to their dining room off to the right side of the house. A deep red rug stretched across most of the room. The dark dining table draped in a delicate white tablecloth took up the center of the room. A multi-armed chandelier hung from the blue ceiling with gold accents, lighting the waiting table setting.

Daniel pulled out a chair at the center of the table for Evelyn before taking the seat on her left. Edith stole the seat on her right, leaving her parents to circle to the other side to face the younger people.

No one said anything as two maids brought out the beginning course of soup. Even though Evelyn couldn't name what it was, the smooth warmth of the liquid eased her tight throat.

She didn't miss the looks Daniel's parents traded as they sipped spoonfuls of soup. She focused on her bowl, pretending to be oblivious to their discomfort.

"I realize everything has happened rather...quickly," Mrs. Prindall spoke up. "But have you thought about the wedding yet, dear? Like your preferences and such?"

"I haven't thought about it at all," Evelyn admitted. "The engagement happened only a few minutes ago. I'm still getting over the shock."

"So it was unexpected for you too?" Mrs. Prindall's smile softened.

"Yes, quite, but I'm happy nonetheless." She looked at Daniel, who also smiled warmly at her.

"There's time to sort out details," Edith spoke up. "You aren't planning to have an engagement as short as your courtship, are you?"

Evelyn hesitated. Did Daniel already have this planned? Clearly, he had considered their future enough to propose, but she had barely thought that far.

"Yes, that's something that needs to be sorted out," Mrs. Prindall agreed. "There are announcements to be made. Invitations to be sent. We have to decide if you'll be having it at our church or yours so we can request the date. I would recommend ours, if I may. The interior is simply divine. These are all things we need to sort out sooner rather than later."

"No matter. Enjoy the feeling of being engaged for a moment," Edith broke in over her mother's words.

Evelyn nodded, grateful for her friend acting as a barrier, but her heart was already racing with Mrs. Prindall's words.

"I promise once we've discussed anything, you'll be the first to know," Daniel told his mother. "Now that the engagement is out of the way, I intend to have plenty of long talks with my fiancée, and we can sort out dates and such then."

When he smiled at her again, her fears dissipated a little bit. If he didn't have their future all planned out in his mind, they could build a vision together. Just the two of them. There was time yet for her to explore this new stage of life thrust upon her, but for once in her life, Evelyn wouldn't be figuring things out alone.

CHAPTER 9

As the pastor's voice boomed through the small sanctuary, Evelyn's focus was on her engagement ring. Due to the size of the diamond, she had considered leaving it at home to avoid attracting unwanted attention—and because she feared losing it—but in the end, she kept it on. It didn't seem right to take it off.

Since Daniel had ushered her straight home after dinner with his parents on Friday, he returned on Saturday for the promised long talk about the wedding. They started in her sitting room, but when Prudence kept jumping in the middle of their discussion with her own ideas, they took a walk to catch a moment alone. The six-month engagement they settled on brought Evelyn some measure of comfort. Long enough to plan for a wedding and adjust to this new idea of marriage, but short enough to prevent the prolonging of anticipation.

"I never thought I'd be the type to rush into marriage, but one night with you was enough to know I never wanted to live without you."

Daniel's sweet words from the walk filled her memory. For the millionth time since the proposal, she wondered if any of this was real, but the ring on her finger was a tangible confirmation that it was.

Before she realized what was happening, the congregation stood for the final hymn. She mumbled through the familiar chorus, trying to force her mind back on the here and now.

After the last note rang out over the room, a flock of women descended on the pew where Evelyn sat with her family.

"Let me see the ring," Claire squealed.

Older women directed their questions toward Prudence about how long Evelyn had been courting, if the date was set, and the venue of the ceremony.

"Of course, it has to happen here, doesn't it?" one silver-haired woman asked.

"I think it's a crime not to marry in your home church." Prudence shot a glance at Evelyn out of the corner of her eye. "But that's something that still needs to be discussed."

"The only thing we have planned so far is that we'll have a six-month engagement," Evelyn spoke up.

Claire squeezed Evelyn's hand. "I'm so happy for you." She lowered her voice as she stared Evelyn in the eye. "Is he a good man?"

Evelyn smiled. "He is a very good man."

Claire hugged her tight. "Good."

As she pulled back from the pastor's wife, Evelyn caught sight of August a few yards away, watching the bustle of the church women. She offered a small wave before another woman's question pulled her attention back to the crowd around her.

"Where will you live?" The woman's pencil-thin gray eyebrows arched toward her church hat.

"Daniel has plenty of money," Prudence jumped in. "I'm sure they'll have a new house."

Evelyn frowned at Prudence, but her stepmother didn't seem to notice as she continued to answer questions as if the wedding was her own, questions Evelyn and Daniel hadn't even discussed—the size of the guest list, the colors of the wedding, the gifts they may need for starting their new life.

"I suppose congratulations are in order."

Evelyn whirled in surprise to find August standing behind her. "Pardon?"

He motioned to her left hand. "Congratulations on the engagement."

"Oh. Yes." She covered the ring with her right hand. "Thank you."

He tilted his head, spinning his straw hat in his hands. "I don't remember you mentioning a beau."

She winced, a strange niggle of guilt pricking her chest. "It was all rather sudden. The courtship. The engagement. I'm still processing it myself."

"I suppose I would have known about it if I bothered to actually listen to the church gossip my sister-in-law brings home each week." He gave a small shrug of his shoulders.

She studied his expression, wondering if what she saw lurking in his brown eyes was disappointment. Surely it wasn't.

"The most important thing is that you'll be free." His attention wandered over her shoulder to her stepfamily.

"Yes, it's exactly how I wanted it."

His face softened into a smile. "Good."

A young woman in a soft pink dress slipped up to August's side, and Evelyn recognized her as a newer church member whom she hadn't become acquainted with yet.

"Shall we be going?" She touched August's elbow. Her gaze flitted between Evelyn and him. "The roast is waiting in the oven, and I don't want it to dry out. You will be joining us, won't you?"

When the young woman turned the question on Evelyn, she gave August a startled look.

August cleared his throat, patting the woman's hand. "I

hadn't exactly gotten around to that part, Mary. Before I realized you were otherwise engaged, I had asked my sister-in-law if I could invite you to Sunday dinner. A trunk that I lost in transit from Ireland finally arrived. It contained all of my photographs and mementos from my trips, and since you love my books so much, I thought you might enjoy seeing them."

Evelyn opened her mouth to thank him for thinking of her, but before the words could leave her lips, Prudence looped her arm through Evelyn's. "All right, dear. We must hurry home to begin planning."

"That does sound like a wonderful afternoon," Evelyn admitted to August. "I regret that I have to decline the offer."

August inclined his head. "I understand."

"See you ladies next week." Prudence waved at the other church ladies before dragging Evelyn toward the aisle, unaware of her ongoing conversation.

Evelyn only had time to offer a brief goodbye to August before Prudence hauled her from the pew, and they joined her father waiting at the back of the sanctuary. The threesome stepped outside to the hired carriage where her stepsisters already sat.

She squeezed into the carriage next to them as her father and stepmother took the opposite seat. While the carriage pulled out of the church lot, she looked out the small window. August emerged from the church with his sister-in-law, and his gaze followed the carriage as he donned his straw Panama hat.

Evelyn sat back in the seat, disappointment sinking like a weight in her chest. It would have been improper for her to accept August's invitation, but she still wished she could have gone. Listening to his glorious tales of travel sounded worlds better than wedding planning with her stepmother.

Evelyn stared at her reflection in the full-length mirror as she held the dress to her shoulders. How long had she been engaged? Two weeks? Three? It felt like a lifetime, but for a moment, she forced herself to slow her thoughts enough to take in the reality of holding a wedding dress up to her frame.

Looking into her own eyes, she whispered the words that hadn't sunk in yet: "I'm a bride."

Running her hand down the silk arm of the ivory sleeve, she fingered the twirling lace around the cuff. "I'm a bride."

Seeing herself behind her mother's wedding dress, she could almost believe it.

"It's a beautiful dress," Edith commented from the end of Evelyn's bed.

Evelyn turned to face her, still holding the dress in place. "But your mother was right. It's too old-fashioned."

Edith cocked her head, her gaze combing over every inch of the fabric. "The waistline is lower than the dresses we looked at this morning, but I think it will compliment your figure. We could change the lace or do something with ribbon to make it more modern. That way it's your mother's dress but with a modern touch suiting a Prindall bride."

"No, I shouldn't entertain the idea. The order has already been placed." Evelyn laid the dress across the trunk at the foot of her bed.

"But obviously, you aren't completely satisfied with what you picked," Edith pressed. "Or else you wouldn't have pulled this out the moment you came home. The order can be canceled."

"But your mother already promised to pay. How could I be so rude?" Evelyn chewed on her lip, but she couldn't take her eyes off her mother's dress.

"You didn't have to accept her offer to pay for it."

Evelyn groaned as she sunk onto the edge of the bed. "Didn't I? It startled me when she started talking about the eyes of

Boston being on this wedding. No dress my family can afford will be worthy of that."

"What did you expect? Every social journalist has been speculating about who Daniel would marry since he was a schoolboy. My brother is the sole heir of my father's fortune and enterprise. Marrying him practically makes you the queen of Boston."

Evelyn clamped her hands over her ears. "Please stop. I hadn't thought that far at all."

Evelyn stared at her mother's dress. Her heart pounded as her fingers found the necklace at her throat, desperately gripping the familiar cross. Every time she went in public with Daniel, it was hard to miss the eyes that followed them. Even if she pretended otherwise, she heard the whispers in the middle of theater shows and art halls, swapping opinions of the unknown girl by Daniel's side. Still, the vision she built was of an intimate wedding, shared with their families and only a few close friends. A moment where the two of them could vow before God the love she had dreamed of since girlhood. Nowhere in her vision had she factored in the eyes of Boston.

"I can't wait to see everyone in my mother's circle when they see who Daniel finally chose to marry." Edith smirked. "Those women have been shoving their daughters under his nose for years. Even an English duchess tried to catch his eyes, but he picked the best one of all." She draped her arm around Evelyn's shoulders. "And I'm here to help any way I can to make this the wedding of your dreams."

"I think I'll need your aid more than I realized. Thank you, by the way, for insisting on my opinion in the dress shop. Prudence and Mrs. Prindall were talking so much that I didn't know what to do."

"Mother can have firm opinions, but I'll teach you how to hold your own. Though Prudence—" Edith winced. "I wish I could help you with that, but now I understand why you spent so much time at my house."

"If the public expects so much from this wedding, is there more expected of me once I'm married?" Evelyn bit her lip when she realized how dumb the question was. Of course, there would be expectations. Why had she never thought about the meaning of marrying a Prindall before? Maybe because it was nothing more than a fanciful daydream only a month ago.

"Well..." Edith drew the word out. "You will be the keeper of his estate, possibly the designer as well, depending on where he decides to live. My mother designed the interior of our house when she and Father married. Father has always said the factories are his business and the house is hers. Then, of course, people will expect plenty of parties and balls to see your new home. That's also how you two will establish yourself in society outside of my family's canopy. I'm sure you'll be invited to tea parties and ladies' events, and that will be your best chance at making alliances that can benefit Daniel with his business. Even though I hate those parties, I can try to help prepare you and accompany you."

"Why do you hate those?" Evelyn swallowed.

"They're supposed to be pleasant social events. However, they're nothing but a breeding ground for gossip and cliques."

Evelyn nodded slowly as she tried to let all the information sink in. "Is that all?"

"I'm sure you're already learning this part, but people will look for you at every event. Theater shows, operas, clubs, art exhibits. Once you bear the Prindall name, women everywhere will be looking at your fashion choices, but I'll be more than happy to help with that as well. I think we've managed to impress everyone so far."

Evelyn chewed on her lip as she flopped back on the bed. She fixed her gaze on the ceiling while the thoughts flew through her mind. She didn't know the first thing about high society, and she never realized how much she was taking on by saying yes to Daniel. What if she couldn't keep up? What if her decisions disappointed him and the elites scrutinized her every move?

Edith rested a hand on Evelyn's shoulder, pulling her from her whirlwind of thoughts. "Evelyn, you look pale. Please don't feel overwhelmed. I'll teach you what you need to learn before the wedding."

"You're a true friend," Evelyn whispered before dragging herself upright.

She picked up her mother's dress to return to the wardrobe, but she paused to stare at the length of ivory satin once more. She tried to picture her mother, young and healthy, in the dress, preparing to marry her father.

What she wouldn't give to have her mother back, for even a moment. How could a girl plan her wedding, plan her future, and face all of these major changes without the guiding presence of a loving mother?

Evelyn's eyes misted over, but she blinked it away as she hung the dress in the wardrobe.

Realizing the late hour of the day, Edith announced her departure with a promise to return another day to begin their etiquette lessons. After seeing her friend out the front door, Evelyn returned to the solitude of her room. The lingering ache for her mother's presence drew her toward her writing desk. Her journal waited in the center of the desk from the night before with an unopened letter on top that had arrived at the same time as Edith. Evelyn picked up the letter, holding her breath as she stared at her name and address written across the front of the envelope in bold, angular strokes.

It had become a nightly habit to sit at her desk with her journal before turning in, and with each night, the habit stretched later. The act of losing herself in a world beyond her own, living an adventure through the eyes of another, was like a balm for her turbulent emotions. She had learned to let go of the tension from a full day of wedding planning with her future in-laws and stepmother by losing herself in another world built of her own words. Every time she came out of her little world, August's praise and encouragement for her little story would replay in her mind until she found herself wishing for his opinion on what she had come up with since he read it.

So after obtaining his brother's address from Claire at church, in a fit of courage that melted away the second the letter was in the post box, Evelyn had copied and sent August the next segment of Rose Wheelock's adventure.

Evelyn stared at her name on the envelope for a moment more before turning it over to rip into the top. She held her breath as she expected to draw out a simple note, something short and dismissive for her unsolicited manuscript, but instead, she unfolded a page filled with his strong handwriting. His warm voice rumbled in her mind as she read the words he penned.

Dear Evelyn,

Thank you for allowing me to read more of your story. I'm afraid I'm invested now, and you better keep the installments coming until Rose's story is complete. You can't leave me without knowing the end.

A surreal euphoria swept over Evelyn as she read further down his letter. After his initial praise for the story, he commented on specific sections he liked or things he thought could be improved. Even his critiques were worded in a way that encouraged her to keep writing.

You have a gift, Evelyn. A gift of beautiful words and captivating storytelling. It would be a shame if you didn't continue to foster it, and someday, I think you should share it with the world. Someday, your name may be on the cover of a book next to mine in stores.

Evelyn let out a long breath as she skimmed over the end of his letter, where he listed a couple of publishers she could submit to. Publishers? She barely had the courage to share this little story with August, let alone the world, but the more she dwelled on the idea, the more excitement simmered in her belly until her heart pounded in her ears.

Shaking herself out of the intense image, Evelyn stuffed the letter back into its envelope and banished it to the corner of her desk. August didn't understand the magnitude of his suggestion, and on the heels of the stress of her upcoming wedding, it was too much to think about.

Deliberately blocking the thoughts of publishing from her mind, Evelyn picked up her pencil and opened the journal to where she had left off. She centered her thoughts on her mother and allowed herself to believe Mother was the only one listening as she began to scratch words onto the paper. Everything else pressing in her life faded away as she escaped to the adventure far outside the borders of her attic room.

CHAPTER 10

Evelyn pulled the white glove over her fingers but paused when she noticed her hands trembling. No matter how hard she tried to concentrate and stop the tremors, she couldn't. After jamming her hand the rest of the way into the glove, she buried them into the folds of her chiffon dress so Daniel wouldn't notice from the seat next to her.

She gazed out the automobile window to distract herself, but as the looming theater drew near, her chest tightened until she feared her lungs might pop from the pressure.

A million thoughts twirled like a cyclone in her mind. The floral arrangements they had yet to finalize. The green fabric for the bridesmaids' dresses that Prudence insisted on while her own preference insisted on another. Edith's last-minute rushed socialite lesson as she piled Evelyn's hair onto her head for their theater date. As if any lessons would fix the hopeless mess Evelyn was proving to be in higher society. She had already failed to properly address a lord and lady once that day. How was she supposed to know they could encounter British nobility at an art museum in Boston?

"Are you ready, dear?" Daniel held out his hand as the automobile came to a stop in front of the theater steps. Men and women dripping in finer cloth and jewels than Evelyn had ever known ascended the steps arm in arm.

Evelyn stared at his gloved fingers before lightly resting hers on top. She could only pray the fabric between their skin was enough to disguise the clamminess of her palms.

As he helped her out of the vehicle, she tried to focus on the confident, calming strength of his fingers wrapped around hers. She straightened her skirts and lifted her chin under his watchful smile. He transferred her hand to his elbow with a pat before leading her forward.

No matter how much she felt like an alien in these clothes, the basic fact remained that Daniel had chosen her. He chose her knowing she was a factory manager's daughter, not an heiress.

Evelyn tried to channel those reassuring thoughts into every step as they ascended the steps together in the same stream as the other high-class attendees. Perhaps Daniel didn't expect the same things from her as everyone else. No matter if anyone else whispered behind their fans about her clumsy manners, she was still his bride-to-be. Maybe, just maybe, if she made it through the wedding, she could breathe easier. Things would slow down enough for her to match her pace to that of high society, and through it all, Daniel would be there holding her hand.

They entered the buzzing foyer, and despite the burning stares from every side, Evelyn kept her focus ahead of her. No matter how many calming thoughts she offered herself to bury the frazzled nerves, the weight of the expectations of those around her seemed to remain a vise grip on her lungs.

Was she about to trade the suppression of her stepmother for the suppression of high society?

Her grip tightened on Daniel's arm.

～

Evelyn rubbed her temples as she stared at the piles of napkins in front of her.

"I don't think ecru is in season." Prudence practically turned her nose up at a napkin held by Mrs. Prindall that looked the same as half the others in consideration.

"It doesn't matter what is in season," Mrs. Prindall dismissed. "Who decides what is in fashion? It's events like these that make the season. We decide what we like, and the rest of society will have a new fad."

"I'm partial to something with more color." Edith picked through the reds, greens, and golds.

"But the napkin color must match the seals on the place-holders," Mrs. Prindall commented. "Do you really want something so wild? Don't forget the floral arrangements that make up the centerpiece."

Evelyn shoved her hands under the table as the trembling of her fingers persisted. Her hands hadn't stopped shaking all week. At this rate, by the time she said "I do," her entire body would be shaking uncontrollably.

"Evelyn, you haven't said much," Prudence snapped without looking at her.

Edith's face washed over with concern. "Evelyn, are you all right? You're as pale as a ghost! Do you need to lie down?"

Evelyn shoved her chair back from the Macarees' table as all eyes turned to her, adding to her panic. "I'm terribly sorry, but I think I need fresh air. Can you ladies handle the napkins while I take a quick walk?"

She didn't wait for a response before fleeing the dining room. She could hear Prudence protesting behind her, but she tuned out her stepmother's voice as she flew out the front door. Blinded to anything happening around her, Evelyn set off down the sidewalk at a brisk, unladylike pace. She didn't care what others might think. She wanted to feel moving air on her face. Anything to distract her from her troubles that kept pace with her no matter how far she walked or how fast she went.

Her legs led her on a distracted journey until she came to the park. Stepping under the canopy of the trees, the quiet haven transported her out of the chaos she left behind.

Breathing deep to return air to her constricted lungs, Evelyn wandered deeper into the oasis. The fresh air acted as an antidote for the stresses of the wedding planning, and the longer she basked in it, the more the tension dissolved from her shoulders. Habit drew her toward the familiar pond.

As if in a vision of déjà vu, Evelyn was surprised to find August there again. This time he had traded his picnic blanket for a nearby bench, but he relaxed in the same brown suit, his straw hat resting on his knee, allowing the breeze to play with tendrils of his hair. He seemed completely transported by the book in his hand, and for a moment, the scene before Evelyn transported her to the last time she sat and talked with him. A time before Daniel proposed and her world turned on end.

A duck stood a few feet away from August, eyeing a paper bag in his lap as if trying to decide if it could steal it without his notice. As she approached, he didn't so much as lift his head, and she had a feeling the duck could steal the bag if it dared to try.

"Hello," she announced herself.

He glanced up, but his surprise melted into a welcoming smile. "Hello, soon-to-be Mrs. Prindall."

Her skin prickled at the sound of the name, and heat rushed to her face. "May I?" She motioned to the bench, fearing her knees may buckle if she didn't.

"Please." He scooted over slightly to allow her an appropriate amount of space.

"You have a friend already. I didn't want to impose." She glanced at the duck as she sat. He had backed away but not given up.

"Ah, I'm afraid I got distracted while feeding him." August set the book between them before opening the bag. The duck waddled closer with a quack. "It's been a while since I've so captured by a good book."

He tossed the expectant duck several bread crumbs before tossing more into the pond, where its kinsmen swam in circles. Once they took notice of the bread, they turned their attention to August as well.

"What brings you here?" August asked as he held a piece of bread toward her.

She took it and pieced it to feed their audience. "I needed a break from wedding planning."

"Is that going well?"

She focused all her attention on tearing the bread into even portions. "Well enough." The short response sounded flat even to her ears.

When she dared a glance at August, he was watching her with lowered brows.

"I got overwhelmed," she whispered. "There is so much more to planning a wedding than I ever imagined. So much more to Daniel's life. I'm not complaining. I just... I needed a moment to myself."

They lapsed into silence as they tossed the remaining bread into the water for the happy ducks. The one who had waited for August's attention joined his friends in the water when he realized that's where most of the bread was going. Evelyn watched the little creatures dart to and fro, their tails wagging with every piece they gobbled.

"Are you as happy as you imagined you would be?"

August's question caught her off guard, but he watched her with the same open expression he had the last time they had met in this park, when she had poured out the loss of her mother to him. No judgment or opinions. Just an eagerness to wait and listen for her to share what she dared.

"This is what I've always dreamed of," she admitted. "More than I ever thought I'd be lucky enough to get."

"So I guess that means you're happy."

She returned her attention to the ducks. "It's different than I imagined, but I'm sure once this whirlwind of newness settles down, it'll be good." She pressed her lips together. "I'm not answering your question, am I?"

He shrugged one shoulder. "I suppose it's not a simple question to answer."

"I'm not naive enough to think reality will always match my dreams. I know some things will be different from what I expected. I need to adjust to them sooner rather than later."

A shadow seemed to descend over August's expression as he turned his focus to the ducks again. He threw the last of the bread into the water before leaning back on the bench, his brows lowered as if deep in thought.

Evelyn threw the last piece of her bread to the first duck and then brushed the crumbs from her cotton skirt.

"Have you written any more of your story?" He broke the silence between them as he clasped his hands behind his neck and cocked his leg out at a casual angle. "I've been trying to patiently wait for the next bit, but the anticipation is building."

She closed her eyes, feeling a little piece of her deflating. "Truthfully, I haven't written in a couple of days. Before then, I was writing every day, sometimes for hours on end, because it helped me forget about the stress of my wedding, but these last few days... the stress has become too much. It feels like it's choking my thoughts so that I can't focus on my story."

"I see." He nodded slowly, his face darkening further.

"I plan to send you the next bit when I'm finished, but I'm not sure when that will be." She cleared her throat, growing uncomfortable with the focus solely on her. "What about you? You mentioned last time that you had some ideas for your next story. Have you started it?"

She was startled as he abruptly stood and paced a few feet away, sending the ducks wading further into the pond. He stood with his back to her, his arms behind his back as he circled one hand around the other wrist. The other hand tightened into a fist. Had she offended him?

His fisted fingers eased open before he turned on his heels to face her again.

"I'm sorry. I shouldn't have pried—" she started, but he shook his head.

"I can't write." He stated the words with finality, his voice gruff and low.

She snapped her mouth shut as she stared at him. "What do you mean you can't write?"

"I haven't been able to write a single word since I left Ireland." His fingers trembled as he wiped a hand over his mouth before returning them behind his back. "When I returned, I didn't know if I would ever write again. When I told you that our conversations had sparked some ideas in me, I wasn't lying. Those were the first ideas I've had since I finished my last book, but I can't seem to flesh anything out on a page."

She tried to process his words as he moved to sit on the bench again. He sat on the edge, his elbows braced on his knees, and she could see the bunched tension of his shoulder muscles through his jacket.

"Are you going to give up writing then?" Her heart constricted at the thought. No more Howard Knightly? His books had been something she looked forward to, and the thought of that ending was almost too much.

"I don't know." He let out a deep breath. "What else is there for me but writing? I've devoted my entire life to this singular pursuit."

She bit her lip as her heart stirred at his words. Isn't that how she felt about Daniel? She'd spent her whole life dreaming of the moment he would fall in love with her. She couldn't imagine the possibility of it failing her now.

"This is all I ever wanted," August continued, but it felt like he took the words right out of her mind. "From my youth, all I ever wanted was to be a successful author. I dreamed of writing books that would grace store shelves. I wanted my name to be known around the world, and I devoted everything to accomplishing that. While all my friends married, attended college, and began their careers, I was writing. I was stepping foot on my first steamer to cross the ocean in pursuit of an adventure on which to base my stories. I couldn't go a day without writing, and I spent all of my money on postage to mail my ramblings to publisher after publisher after publisher." He shook his head, closing his eyes. "Even when my family doubted me, I didn't let anything steer me off course. I was so sure that I was meant to be a world-renowned author."

"And you did," Evelyn broke in. "You proved that your dreams were true, and you became successful. What went wrong?"

"I sacrificed everything, including my health. I told you I fell sick in Ireland, but it was worse than that. I fell sick, and when I could have rested and recovered quickly, I pushed myself to finish my book on time for my editors. A simple sickness became pneumonia in both of my lungs that nearly took me to my deathbed, all in the name of proving that I was great. Then I was alone, fighting for my life in a hospital room in a foreign land, far from anyone I knew or loved. I don't think I've ever been given as much time to reflect on my life as I did during those times."

"I'm so sorry," she whispered as she rested her hand over his. His fingers trembled beneath her touch. "But I'm glad you survived and recovered."

He dropped his gaze to the grass between his shoes. "My lungs have recovered, but I have not. I don't know if I'll ever be the same again. I realized in my hospital bed how exhausted I was. How lonely. Worn out. Even when I was fighting for my life, I had to field off an endless stream of letters and telegrams from my publisher, talking about the release of *Peril on the Cliffs of Moher* and asking about my next project. Just the thought of picking up a pen again repulsed me. I came to a point where I despised everything I ever loved about writing. All I could think about was the pressure of sales numbers, the looming presence of my publisher, and the demand to make something bigger and better than the last. I hated all of it. It was all meaningless."

His shoulders deflated as he buried his face in his hands, and Evelyn's heart crumbled at the broken man beside her. What happened to the warm, confident author she had grown affectionate of in such a short time?

He straightened with a long inhale, schooling his features into a neutral expression. "Once I recovered from my sickness, I sent my publisher a short missive informing them that I would be on vacation for a bit, and then I set sail for Boston. I didn't even tell them that's where I was going. I wanted to get away from everything."

Evelyn bit her lip as she stared across the pond. Empathy drove her to find something to say, to offer some kind of encouragement or comfort, but what could she say?

August broke the silence between them with a short chuckle, and a small smile lifted his lips. "What a pair we make today, don't we? Both trying to navigate our lifelong dreams while being slowly crushed alive by them."

"I'm not being crushed by mine." If that was true, why did the trembling of her hands match his? "I'm just adapting to the reality of them."

His smile wiped away as he nodded and focused on the ground again. "Perhaps this is why I've been so interested in your writing. It makes my soul yearn for the early days of my own writing journey when everything I penned came from the heart and was untouched by the world's influence. I don't want to pressure you into something you aren't interested in pursuing, but I truly believe all of the good things I've told you about your story so far. I believe in the heart I see in your writing. Someone out there needs your story."

Her gaze wandered to the pond and the ducks that had drifted even further away. His words stirred a feeling in her spirit she couldn't quite identify. She tried to picture herself finishing and publishing her little story someday, but the image didn't seem to fit in with the idea of her future with Daniel. Could the two coincide?

As her life stood now, writing was a comfortable pursuit. It felt right in the few hours of the day she had to herself to pretend to be telling her mother a story, carrying herself away on an adventure she could never live. It bridged a connection between the warm memories of her past and her wistful ideas of the future. But the thought of sharing that with the world brought a twisting feeling to her stomach.

"I'm not sure about publishing." She rubbed her palms on her skirt as she straightened her back. "I'm not sure it's for me, but if nothing else, I'll send you a copy of my story when I finish it. I will finish it, sooner or later. I need to know how it ends too. Maybe you and I are the only ones who need it."

He gave a small shrug with a nod. "I can live with that if that's what you want."

Evelyn focused on the pond again. The ducks had dispersed, giving up hope for any more bread. Without invitation, thoughts about the wedding plans awaiting her loomed over her mind like a shadow, and she realized she had already been away from home too long. Despite the reluctance weighing her limbs, she stood from the bench.

"I should return home before Edith worries and sends a search party after me. I left rather abruptly."

"I wish you the best of luck in that wedding planning." He stood to doff his straw hat to her.

"Thank you." She turned to leave but only took two steps before her thoughts stilled her feet. Without allowing herself the chance to second guess, she whirled around to face him again. "I don't want to pressure you into something you don't want either. I don't want you to return to something that will run you into the ground, but if you aren't ready to give up your writing, I think you need to know that there are still people who need your story too."

He raised his eyebrows in surprise, but before he could respond, she said, "I told you when we first met that your stories meant the world to me because they brought the world to me, and I meant it. There are plenty of people who need your books to escape on an adventure for a time. People who need you to show them how to dream, how to be brave, how to live each day with a daring spirit. I pray that God will show you that and that He will heal you, not just in body, but in mind. The world would be a much dimmer place without your beautiful words to bring it to life."

He continued to stare at her in shock, but she turned on the heels and hurried away before he could say anything. Her cheeks burned with the unfettered honesty she had spilled to him, but her heart settled with a peace that told her she had spoken what needed to be said. Maybe her words wouldn't change how he felt, but she couldn't let him give up writing without knowing how much it touched the lives of those who read his stories.

She didn't slow her pace until she reached the edge of the park. Almost like crossing a barrier, the moment she stepped foot out of the park a heaviness settled over her chest again. All of the pressing wedding details and her insecurities about adapting to Daniel's life flooded back into her mind like a tidal wave. She tried to return her focus to thoughts of a peaceful future full of love at Daniel's side, but the pressing issues distorted the beautiful image.

August was ready to walk away from writing, his lifelong dream. What would happen if she simply walked away?

The thought nearly stole her breath and tightened her lungs even further. She tried to banish it before it would overwhelm her, replacing it with Daniel's handsome face. How could she think about walking away? Of leaving him and never looking back? Her heart had been tangled up with him since girlhood, and untangling it might tear it to pieces.

Evelyn steeled her nerves as she made her way through the streets toward her family's home. She would do exactly as she told August she would: she would learn to adapt her childhood dreams to the reality that was before her now, but she would not lose them. She would cling to them as if her life depended on it. She would believe and hope in them until she saw her own "happily ever after," and she would pray that August could do the same with his.

<h1 style="text-align: center;">CHAPTER 11</h1>

"What is this?" Evelyn blinked at the automobile as she descended the steps from her family's home. "I thought we were meeting at the restaurant."

"I wanted to escort my lady to dinner personally." Daniel held her hand as he led her around the automobile. He opened the passenger door with a flourish of his free hand. "I thought we could use some time alone before joining our families."

Her cheeks warmed as he winked, and she slid into the seat hoping he wouldn't notice. After shutting her door, Daniel circled the vehicle to take his place behind the steering wheel. Evelyn adjusted the feathered stole around her shoulders, trying to hold in a sneeze. Edith had said something about fashion and making a statement when she pressed the ridiculous accessory upon Evelyn, and of course, Evelyn complied.

"Are your parents on their way?" Daniel asked as he turned onto the cobbled road.

"They'll be leaving soon." Evelyn gripped the edge of the seat as they rattled their way through town.

Nerves played in her stomach like they had from the moment Prudence and Mrs. Prindall suggested a family dinner.

Both of their families. Together. It seemed like a bad idea to Evelyn, but the two women insisted. What would their families possibly have to bond over? Her father was Mr. Prindall's employee, not equal. Not to mention, the last time she had dined in public with the Prindalls, she managed to garner frowns from Mrs. Prindall and kicks under the table from Edith over her improper dinner etiquette. She made mistakes about spoons and napkins and so many other things that it made her head spin. Her whole family was likely to follow in her mistakes.

Evelyn didn't realize Daniel was talking about his work until she had already missed most of what he said. He was saying something about the growth of the business in time for him to take more responsibility. She tried to listen harder to catch up in the conversation, and she hoped if she missed something important he would think the road noise prevented her from hearing.

"Don't say anything yet, but my father confided in me today that he wants to make your father district manager for the good work he's done for our company," Daniel commented as he shifted the car into another gear with a jerk that sent Evelyn's heart into her throat.

After a moment, the news sunk in, and she blinked. A district manager? Wasn't it only a few weeks ago her father complained Mr. Prindall barely paid him any attention? Was it really her father's hard work that moved Mr. Prindall to promote him? Surely, Mr. Prindall wouldn't do it out of shame for his son having a lowly father-in-law.

"Doesn't that please you?" Daniel darted a worried look her way.

It wasn't until his gaze dipped to her hands that she realized she was twisting the pinky of her glove. She forced her hands to relax. "No, no, that's wonderful for my father. I hope I don't slip up and say something over dinner."

"I'll try to intervene if you do." He grinned. "But I'm afraid I'm in the same danger. I couldn't even keep myself from telling you."

She offered a weak smile before turning her gaze to the window. This was wonderful for her father. It truly was. Even if the entire reason for the promotion was her, wasn't that okay? A promotion was a promotion, and her father was long overdue.

But if his promotion was based on her, what happened if she displeased her future in-laws? Would they go so far as to take away what they generously gave to her family? As her stomach twisted, threatening to heave despite its emptiness, she could understand how August came close to walking away from his writing for good. Running far away felt like the easiest solution to the pressure of expectations.

A fleeting thought flew through her mind: *Is this worth it?*

Her heart raced, and her head grew light.

"Daniel," she choked out.

"Yes?" He glanced her way with a smile.

She stared at him as she tried to bring some rational thought back to her mind. Every day the expectations of being his bride seemed to grow, and things she never thought she'd have to think about chased through her thoughts. She focused on the outline of his features in the fading sunlight to remind herself of what she always considered when she felt overwhelmed. He had chosen her, and no matter what came her way as she tried to join his world, he would be there for her.

"Why do you wish to marry me?" Her words came out light like a wisp, and shame seared through her for such an insecure question. But she needed to hear it.

Confusion flashed over his face before he smiled again. "My mother warned me about this. Pre-wedding anxieties are hitting already? If it eases your fears, you captivated me from the moment I laid eyes on you. Then I got to know you and saw your sweet disposition that is fitting for a wife."

She wanted to swoon under his sweet words. She willed them to be enough to calm her fears, but the anxiety continued to roar in her ears.

"Thank you," Evelyn whispered.

He seemed to sense the tension still radiating from her as his smile faded. "Why are you asking? It is just pre-wedding anxieties, isn't it?"

"Yes, I think so." She licked her dry lips and forced herself to swallow. "Truthfully, everything has been much harder than I anticipated."

His brows scrunched. "What do you mean?"

"It feels like we come from different worlds. I'm learning a whole new manner of how to dress, talk, and eat. There are things I'm expected to do, like hosting parties and running an estate, that I don't know the first thing about. There's so much more I have yet to learn, and I'm beginning to worry I won't be able to." Some of the tension in her chest eased as the words spilled from her mouth. The honesty acted as a balm for her frayed soul.

"Isn't Edith helping you learn these things?"

"Well, yes, but—"

"Then I'm sure you'll learn in time. With her help, you'll be able to master whatever you don't know already. It can't be any different than school lessons that take time and practice to learn. As I thought, these are pre-wedding anxieties, but tonight we aren't mingling with society. It's only family. Try to relax and forget about all of that."

She sank back into the seat, the tension returning. Her mind screamed that he didn't understand. His family *was* high society. She still needed to think, talk, and eat just right.

Why didn't his answer calm her like she expected? Voicing her fears was supposed to make her feel better, and then he was supposed to offer sweet words to calm all her worries. He had even indulged her by telling her why he loved her. Any woman would be thrilled to hear such words from a privileged young man like him. Of all the young women at that ball, he chose her as the most beautiful.

But why did his words make her heart sink further?

"Papa, what made you fall in love with Mama?" Eight-year-old Evelyn asked as she reclined in her mother's lap under the shade of the tree. Their finished picnic meal sat on the blanket around them.

Edwin smiled at his wife, his eyes seeming to drink in every inch of her face. "I have never met a woman of more noble character than your mother. From the moment I met her, grace, beauty, and joy emanated from her. Even though she came from a poor family, she never seemed to lack contentment, and her faith followed her wherever she went. The more I got to know her, the more I came to believe I couldn't live without this woman in my life. She made everything about me better."

Evelyn blinked past the tears at the memory of her father's adoring words. Daniel wished to marry her for her beauty and "sweet disposition that was fitting for a wife." That was the end of it. Neither of them knew each other well enough to know how their personalities would get along. How many endless walks had they been on where it seemed they did nothing but talked? Yet when she tried to think of what they discussed, she could remember nothing. It was all meaningless drivel. They talked about family, but she couldn't tell the true story of how hers treated her. They talked about his work and what filled their days, but what about their future? Their plans? He didn't know anything about her hopes, dreams, or struggles. Perhaps her parents' marriage was too high to hope for, but what would a marriage with Daniel be based on? One dreamlike night. One heart-stopping kiss.

Before she could let her thoughts spiral any deeper, Daniel

pulled the automobile up to the restaurant, and after parking in front of the valet, he came around to open her door.

A numbness washed through her limbs as she took Daniel's arm. At least it was better than the panic. This she could smile through.

They were the last to arrive at the table draped in a pure white tablecloth. Golden candle stands provided a low light that reflected off the fine china setting and full champagne glasses. The table seemed to divide the two sides of Evelyn's life, with her family on one side and her future in-laws on the other. Even as Edith beamed at her outfit, the work of her own hands, her stepsisters wrinkled their noses.

Evelyn sat on the Prindalls' side of the table, between Edith and the end, and Daniel took the seat on the end. With a pasted smile—the one thing she was learning well—Evelyn tried to relax.

Mr. Prindall did the entirety of the ordering for the table, and Prudence did almost the entirety of the talking for the table. She seemed to rattle on about anything that came to mind. The weather, the factories, the wedding details. Whether the Prindalls were charmed by her chatter and large smiles, Evelyn couldn't be sure, but she did her best to keep her own charm throughout.

Even though her heart wasn't in it, she traded smiles with Daniel when appropriate, laughed a light trill with the rest, and listened to Edith's whispered opinions with patience. Maybe she didn't need to understand Daniel's world. Maybe she just needed to learn how to fake her way through, but even as she told herself that, some part of her soul whispered that dreaded question again. *Is it worth it?* But with one look into his blue eyes, she pushed the question out as quickly as it came.

"Dahlia or Florence could stay with you for a spell—after the honeymoon, of course—to help finish the house. Perhaps you can introduce them into society through your parties."

Evelyn looked up from pushing a cooked tomato on her plate, letting her plastered smile slip into a frown. When had the conversation moved on to post-wedding? Prudence grinned at her and Daniel with an expectant look on her face.

"P-pardon?" Evelyn stammered out when she realized Daniel was looking at her too.

"Won't you need help decorating your new estate? And I'm sure you'll need an extra hand or two until you become accustomed to running your own home. Your sisters would be perfect to assist you."

Evelyn bristled at the use of the word "sisters," but before she could correct her stepmother, Prudence continued, "You may want their help for several months if you come to be with child following the honeymoon. You know it can happen as fast as that."

She giggled like it was a silly, scandalous thought, but all Evelyn could do was stare at her with her mouth agape. Edith nudged her knee under the table, and she snapped her teeth together, pressing her lips in a firm line.

"Can you imagine the excitement if there was a birth announcement following behind the wedding?" Mrs. Prindall gasped. "Of course, we don't want it so soon that eyebrows are raised, but it's never too early to think about the next heir."

"And she'll need assistance if it happens that fast."

"My sister lived with us for a time when I was pregnant with Daniel." Mrs. Prindall waved her hand as if finalizing the matter. "Nothing is more comforting to a newly expecting mother than family at hand to help organize and prepare for the new addition."

"We'll have more than enough room if both of you would like to come," Daniel said to Florence and Dahlia. "I would gladly open my doors to you for Evelyn's comfort as she settles into her new home, but as for the matter of a baby, I think it's best to handle those things when they come in their own time."

Even though he kept his tone light, he gave his mother a look that was probably meant to discourage any more daydreaming about grandchildren.

"Splendid!" Prudence clapped. "We can discuss the details and dates of their stay at a later date, but it makes me so happy to know that all of my girls will remain close after Evelyn is married."

Evelyn dropped her fork on her plate and balled her fists in her lap as she stared at Prudence. Her stepmother didn't seem to notice as she gayly swept on to the next topic. Prudence was sorely mistaken if she thought she could follow Evelyn after her marriage. She was marrying Daniel to get away from her sphere of influence, and that included her daughters.

Evelyn lowered her gaze to her plate to avoid causing a scene. Now wasn't the time to put Prudence in her place, but she would. Starting with talking to Daniel to ensure he understood she wanted no part of this scheme involving her so-called sisters. The fact he didn't know how disastrous that would be proved that he didn't know her at all.

Keeping her smile through the rest of the dinner was much harder than in the beginning, and by the time they rose from the table, Evelyn wanted to escape to the solace of her attic room. As much as she knew she needed to have a long talk with Daniel, the exhaustion of the evening caused her to shy away from the idea.

"The evening is still young. Is there somewhere else you would like to go?" Daniel asked as he offered her his arm.

"I'm sorry, but I have a bit of a headache," Evelyn admitted, her gaze flitting to her family, who watched on. Perhaps it was the most truthful thing she had said all night.

His joy visibly diminished, but he nodded. "Then I will deliver you safely home."

"There's no need for you to come all the way. I can go home

with my family." She rose on her toes to brush a kiss on his cheek. "I'll see you tomorrow for our tour of the church."

He didn't try to hide the disappointment in his eyes, but he gave her knuckles a respectful kiss. "Sleep well, and I'll see you tomorrow."

After brushing kisses onto Edith's cheeks in farewell, Evelyn followed her family from the restaurant to their modest carriage. Squeezing next to her stepsisters on the narrow bench, she kept her eyes out the window. Prudence chattered on about the success of the evening, but Evelyn's headache drowned out her stepmother.

As soon as they arrived home, she escaped to her room and deflated against the door after shutting it. She blew out a breath, yanking the satin gloves from her shaking fingers. Thoughts about children and her stepsisters' future visits and a list of wedding details outside of her control ran endless circles in her mind. What happened to a quiet future full of love and peace like she once knew with her parents?

It was her fault Daniel didn't know to defend her against her stepfamily's involvement. She was the one who didn't tell him what happened in the privacy of her family's home. She was the one who allowed Prudence to wiggle into the middle of the wedding plans unopposed. Every time she considered standing up to her, her father's voice played in her head, reminding her to respect her stepmother. Disavowing her in front of her soon-to-be in-laws would cause a ruckus that she didn't have the heart to navigate.

But this was supposed to be her hopeful future, and her conniving stepsisters were nowhere in the picture. How could she handle the situation with grace and respect?

Her gaze traveled to her desk, her fingers itching to pick up her pencil and lose herself in another world. *Mother, what would you do?*

The question went unanswered in the quiet room, and her

growing headache prevented her from trying to untangle the mess of her thoughts anymore. She stepped over to the desk and sank into the chair. When she opened the journal, she stared at the blank space waiting to be filled, but no words formed in her mind.

After several minutes of staring at nothing, she flipped back to the beginning of the journal. She began reading, and even though she only intended to refresh herself on the introductory first paragraph, she found herself going further down the page. Then flipping to the next. And the next.

The troubled twisting in her spirit quieted as she lost herself in the story of Rose Wheelock. Her heart stirred with the rise and falls of the heroine's story. Rose materialized in her mind as she always envisioned her when she wrote: a woman unmoved by the trials of life. One who always faced every new obstacle and hardship with courage and grace. The image emerged as the image of her mother, steadfast and full of faith. Everything she hoped to be in this life.

As she neared the end of what she'd already written, her conversation with August about the purpose of her story crossed her mind. He believed that someone needed her story. She told him maybe it was only them that needed it.

What if she was wrong?

This wasn't only her story, created out of her daydreams. This was her mother's story, albeit loosely. Her mother was a beautiful light, taken from this world too early. What if this was Evelyn's chance to share her with the world? To renew her legacy?

Evelyn's gaze landed on August's letter still banished to the corner of her desk. Was it crazy to consider? When she first read the letter, it was enough to make her heart race and stomach twist, but now, as she stared at it, her thoughts quieted in a way they hadn't all day.

The world would have been a better place if it had the

chance to know Rose Macaree. Maybe someone needed Rose Wheelock instead.

Evelyn pulled a clean paper out of her desk drawer and grabbed her fountain pen and ink. She opened August's letter and found his instructions for submitting to a publisher. Trying not to think about what she was doing, she copied out the first chapter of her story. After she had three neat copies, she penned three separate inquiry letters, each addressed to one of the three publishers August listed in his letter.

After folding each of the letters and sealing them into envelopes, she left the envelopes atop her journal in the center of her desk. She whirled away from the desk and began pulling the pins from her hair.

Maybe she had gone mad. Maybe it was all a mistake. Perhaps all three would respond with scathing rejections, and that would teach her to keep her fanciful stories to herself. Who would want to read her words?

August would.

Evelyn paused with her dress halfway over her head, his glowing words of praise racing through her head. Was it possible someone else could love her story too?

She shed her dress and underthings, trading them for a soft, cotton nightgown. As she crawled under blankets, her eyes were drawn to the envelopes on her desk. When she wrote, she felt at peace. She felt connected with her mother in a way she hadn't since losing her. She felt like she was escaping on her own adventure.

It felt right, but how did that fit into her other dreams? No one said she couldn't be both Daniel's wife and write on the side. Maybe that would be the complete fulfillment of her dreams. She had always wanted love and a family, but her mind constantly wandered to adventure and daydreams. Maybe—just maybe—she could have both.

CHAPTER 12

Evelyn craned her neck to take in the stone arches far above their heads. Bright light filtered through the stained-glass murals that were almost as tall as the arches, and the sound of their shoes on the stones echoed through the great room. The intricate architecture and exquisite design put her family's little wooden church to shame.

Mrs. Prindall and Prudence walked down the center aisle ahead of them, deep in conversation with the pastor about ceremony options. She and Daniel should have been part of the conversation, but she was content to fall behind. She had been waiting since their brunch for a moment alone with him to talk about last night's events.

In the light of a new day, she had easily concluded that all she and Daniel needed was a deep talk with full honesty. She could finally share the truth about her stepfamily. They could talk about their dreams for the future, including details like starting a family. Maybe with more understanding between the two of them, she would find the peace she needed.

Evelyn cleared her throat and hoped their voices wouldn't carry to the group ahead. "Do you want children right away?" It wasn't the topic she was hoping to start with, but in her nervousness, it seemed like the easiest starting point.

Daniel's gaze darted down to her, and he tugged at the collar of his shirt as he looked forward again. "Ah, well, truthfully I hadn't thought about it until last night."

She smiled a little. So he didn't have their future all planned out in his mind.

"I do want children," he rushed on. "If you want them right away, I could easily warm up to the idea, but somehow I imagined having time to settle into married life before we add to our number."

"I agree actually. We're both young. There's no harm in waiting at least a few months or a year before we have children." Her chest warmed with their agreement, and she decided to press forward. "Another thing. I don't want my stepsisters to stay with us. Not after the wedding. Not when I'm pregnant."

He stopped walking, a frown replacing his smile. "I thought this was already decided last night."

She swallowed as her anxious feelings returned. "I'm not comfortable with the idea."

"But you didn't say that last night when it was being discussed."

"I didn't want to create a scene."

"But now we've extended the invitation. Do you know how it will look if I tell them they're not welcome? That will start the relationship with my in-laws off right, I'm sure." He threw his hand in the air with a frustrated shake of his head.

"I'm sorry. I should have said something, but I felt like I couldn't."

"Why don't you want them? Can't you deal with it now that it's decided?"

Evelyn rounded her shoulders, cutting a glance toward the pastor and the two women. Thankfully they were far enough ahead not to notice Daniel and her falling behind. "I thought maybe Edith would have told you about my volatile relationship with my stepfamily—"

"Volatile? This is the first I'm hearing of anything like that."

"—but I suppose she respected my privacy."

"You haven't said anything either. They've been involved in our wedding planning. You've never treated them with anything but kindness. When did things become volatile?"

She pressed her fingers to her temples as his firm words swirling on the edge of anger quickened her heart rate. "I'm sorry. I should've said something sooner, but I don't like to speak badly of anyone, especially the woman my father chose as his wife. But as my future husband, you deserve to know the truth—" She snapped her mouth shut as Mrs. Prindall and Prudence glanced back at them.

Daniel held up a finger to let them know they needed a moment, and then he grabbed Evelyn's arm to turn their backs to the group. "What truth do I need to know?"

Evelyn glanced over her shoulder to see Prudence coming toward them. "Can we please go somewhere private to talk? I'll explain everything, and I think there are some other things we should discuss too."

"And abandon our appointment? The pastor was gracious to offer us time to view the church." He pinched the bridge of his nose. "What other things do you feel like I need to know?"

"Is something the matter?" Prudence spoke up behind them.

Evelyn remained rooted in place as Daniel turned to face Prudence. She closed her eyes and drew in a deep breath. This was not how the conversation was supposed to go.

"I'm sorry. We were discussing something between ourselves." Daniel returned to his normal light tone. "We need a few minutes."

With his hand on her arm again, he guided her to the back of the sanctuary. "Tell me what your stepfamily does to you."

She squeezed her eyes shut, her hands shaking as she clasped them together. Suddenly she found herself at a loss of how to describe half a lifetime of ill-treatment in a moment. "I don't have a good relationship with them. None of them care for me. They order me around like a common maid. My stepmother is unafraid to raise her voice at me or lay her hands on me if I do something she doesn't like." She covered her wrist with her fingers. The bruises were gone, but her skin tingled with the memory of them. "They have mistreated me ever since my father brought them into our house."

Daniel began to pace in front of her, his hands clasped behind his back and his brows knitted together. "Does your father know about this?"

"I don't know. He can't be completely blind to it."

"So he doesn't say anything about it?"

"He asks me to respect Prudence as the woman of the house."

Daniel paused his pacing and blew out a long breath through his nose. "Then that's what we'll do. We will respect her as your stepmother until we're married and you're no longer part of their household. That doesn't exactly solve this issue of your stepsisters' visit and their involvement after we marry, but we'll sort that out later. What else did you want to talk to me about?"

Evelyn gripped her mother's cross as her jaw tightened. The issue of children seemed easy to push off until the right time, but this matter seemed entirely different. However, the dismissive tone he used made her think he wouldn't agree.

"I just realized in all of this that I want to know more about you. There are so many important things we've never talked about. What have you always dreamed of having in a wife? How do you envision your future? I know you want to take over your father's company, but surely there is more to your life than that. What are the secret wishes of your heart that drive you?"

He stared at her like the words coming from her mouth weren't English, his expression growing more and more baffled as she spoke. After she stopped, he blinked.

"Those are the questions you felt couldn't wait?" he sputtered. "We're wasting the pastor's time to talk about... dreams?"

Her gaze flickered to the pastor who watched them from afar—and hopefully out of earshot. Embarrassment shot through her, burning her cheeks. She knew it wasn't the right time to bring it up, but the questions felt like they were going to eat her alive if she didn't voice them.

"Could we go for a walk after this appointment?" she asked past the tightness in her throat.

"I have a meeting with my father. I won't be free until late this evening."

"Maybe now isn't the right time, but these things do matter to me. What if we haven't talked about things that could affect our marriage?"

He paused, his gaze searching her face. He must have seen the anxiety written across her features because his expression softened. After closing the gap between them in one stride, he brushed the back of his fingers on her cheek, sending heat through her skin.

"Nothing is going to come between us. We may have a few things to iron out, but what we have is special. Please don't let the pre-wedding jitters bother you."

He brushed a kiss on her forehead before taking her hand. "Can we agree to put a pause on this discussion and not leave the pastor waiting any longer?"

All ideas of defense died on her tongue, and she merely nodded. He tucked her hand in the crook of his elbow and patted it before pulling her toward the aisle again. Evelyn dropped her gaze to their matching pace, his words circling in her mind.

What did they have? One dreamlike night. One heart-stopping kiss.

What if it wasn't enough?

~

Evelyn sat in a high-backed chair in the Prindalls' sitting room. She clasped her necklace in her fingers, rubbing her thumb over the ridges of the cross. Daniel said that his meetings would last late into the evening, so she would wait. The more she thought about their discussion throughout the day, the more she was sure it wasn't over.

The front door slammed, startling her in her seat. She straightened her spine and tried to listen.

"Good evening, Young Master Prindall. Your fiancée awaits you in the sitting room."

"Thank you," Daniel quietly responded to the butler.

His dress shoes clicked on the polished floor, bringing him to fill the doorway.

"Evelyn." He said her name in a way that sounded like a sigh.

She met his gaze and was surprised to see him in an almost disheveled state. Locks of his golden hair fell over his forehead, no longer controlled by his hair pomade. His tie draped untied around his neck, the top button of his shirt undone. As he raked a hand down his face, her determination wavered.

"I thought we could talk tonight, but would it be better if I came back tomorrow?" she offered, patting the chair next to her.

He dropped into the chair, all of his usual proper posture melting into cushions. "I would rather not have this hanging over my head. What else did you want to discuss? Something about dreams and futures?"

She focused on her ring as she turned it on her finger. "I've done a lot of thinking since our talk this morning, and one thing is clear to me. There are still a lot of things we don't know about each other."

"Of course. Isn't that the point of marriage? To spend the rest of our lives learning each other?"

When he put it that way, she wanted to believe it. To give in, accept his affections as enough, and forget the rest of her worries. But she hadn't spent the whole afternoon thinking about them for nothing.

"Shouldn't we make sure that our priorities and visions for the future line up at least?" she murmured. "Our courtship and our engagement happened so quickly. Perhaps too quickly. What if... what if we took some time to not worry about the wedding and instead focus on getting to know each other, the important things?"

He leaned forward in the chair, frowning. "What do you mean? Can you take time off from planning for that?"

She closed her eyes for a moment. "We could postpone the wedding."

His spine straightened. "Postpone? Do you know how much money has already gone into this wedding? The announcement has gone to the papers. Our mothers have been working so hard. Postponing it would upheave everything."

She clenched her fists at his use of the word "mother" for her stepmother, but he continued his rant with no room for her to interject, "Fast engagements happen all the time. As I said, we will have a lifetime to get to know each other and to sort out the little details about our lives."

"Yes, but what if it isn't only little details we have left to sort? How much have we learned about each other in such a short time?"

"I know everything I need to vow myself to you. I thought you felt the same way, but am I wrong?"

Despite the hardness of his tone, the hurt in his eyes tore at Evelyn's heart, and her determination wavered.

He knew everything about her that he needed? Twenty-four hours before, he didn't even know she was mistreated by her stepfamily. That alone proved there were a lot of things—important things—neither of them knew about the other.

Did he know how strongly she held to the faith her mother instilled in her? Did he know the new dream blossoming in her life through the discovery of writing? Did he know the vision she had crafted of her future from childhood? How could he if they never talked about it?

He knew the historical facts of her life—the death of her mother, the remarriage of her father, and her befriending of Edith—but did he know how she still grieved her mother, how their house was never the same again, or how Edith had become her lifeline in the darkest parts of her life? Shouldn't the man who would soon know her both body and soul know those things too? Or at least show some desire to learn them?

Her tongue refused to move as she stared into Daniel's steady gaze. Something in her desperately screamed that she needed to say yes. Yes, she could vow herself to him right then and there, but the words wouldn't form.

After several seconds of silence, Daniel sighed, dropping his head to rub the back of his neck. "I don't want to fight with you."

At least there was one thing they agreed on. Evelyn kneaded her hands in her lap, fighting to form words in her mind that wouldn't come out a jumbled, emotional mess.

"Maybe the stress of wedding planning has gotten to you." He braced his hands on his knees as he pushed himself to his feet. "Why don't you take a few days off from the wedding? I know my mother was supposed to look at the bridesmaids' dresses with you tomorrow, but I'll let her know that it needs to be postponed. I'll deal with any rescheduling that needs to be done in order for you to have a few days off. Then, when you've had some time to rest, we can readdress all of this." He waved his hand in a circle as if trying to encompass the topic.

When their eyes met, she took in every line of his face, deepened by a tension and tiredness she'd never seen on him before.

Her father's face flashed before her eyes, and suddenly the space between her and Daniel felt achingly familiar.

"Daniel." She couldn't let him walk away with the distance between them, not like how she let her father slip further and further away.

"Go home and rest. I'll tell our driver to take you home." He strode from the room, leaving Evelyn sitting alone in the quiet room. She swallowed as she stood, her hands shaking to the point she could barely hold onto her necklace.

"I know everything I need to vow myself to you. I thought you felt the same way, but am I wrong?"

His words echoed through her mind, making her wince. Her heart wrenched in two as if torn between her feelings and his passionate opinions. Was he—as she already knew him—enough to commit her future to?

No matter how she considered it, every time she saw the future, she saw him, but she couldn't shake the feeling in her core that something was missing.

CHAPTER 13

$\mathcal{E}$velyn buried deeper under her blankets as the front door slammed, signaling her family's departure. Guilt wracked her for missing something as important as church, but when Prudence had pounded on her door to wake her, she couldn't bring herself to leave her bed. She claimed she was too sick, and she truly felt it.

Maybe it wasn't an actual illness so much as lack of sleep, but either way, she couldn't pull herself together for church.

Evelyn dozed for as long as the light in her room allowed, but when it was too bright to ignore, she dragged herself out of bed with blurry eyes and a pounding head. Since her family was gone and Lottie was off for the day, she padded down to the kitchen in her house shoes and nightgown.

She found a bit of bread from the night before in the pantry. She smeared jam on it for a makeshift breakfast. Complete with a glass of milk, the nourishment perked up her energy enough to return to her room to dress.

Dresses spilled out of a trunk in the corner of the room from Edith, but Evelyn bypassed the fine silks and chiffons in favor of one of her old cotton tops and skirts. Not as fashionable, but they felt soft and familiar on her skin.

The sunlight pouring through her window beckoned her to enjoy its warmth. Eying her trunk of books, she decided she felt good enough to venture out.

After braiding her hair, she looked through her trunk before selecting the first Howard Knightly book to reread. Hugging it close, Evelyn snuck out the backdoor of the house, even if the only witness now was One she couldn't hide from.

She took deep breaths as she followed the familiar path to the park she was growing quite fond of. For the first time in what felt like weeks, she could draw a full breath into her lungs without the vice grip of anxiety choking her.

An odd sense of disappointment filled her when she came to the pond and saw no evidence of August. What had she expected? He was most likely in church, where she should have been.

Pushing the condescending thoughts from her mind, she sank onto the bench to read and watch the ducks. As a couple of ducks paused to look her way, she wished she thought to bring the rest of the bread, but that thought only brought her mind back to August. Why couldn't she stop thinking about him?

She closed her eyes. Her thoughts hadn't stopped swirling since she left Daniel's house the night before, and something in her yearned to share her burden with someone else. To spill the painful thoughts her heart was laboring over and receive some sort of advice to quiet the disorder in her soul. Edith was too close to Daniel to be a safe confidant, and her mother was out of reach. But why did her mind go to August?

Evelyn shook herself to snap out of that train of thought, and she cracked open the book to lose herself in Howard Knightly's world. But no matter how hard she stared at the words on the first page, her mind refused to read them.

"Fancy seeing you here."

Evelyn's head shot up to find August standing in front of her in his familiar brown suit but with his hair slicked in place for once. His smile was small and tentative.

"Your stepmother told me you were sick, but I knew it couldn't be too serious when she was more concerned about accomplishing enough wedding planning." He eased onto the bench next to her.

"There will be no wedding planning today," she muttered.

His warm brown eyes searched her face, and she looked away under the heat of his gaze.

"Is everything all right? Has she laid her hands on you again?"

"No," she whispered.

He hesitated. "No to which?"

"No, everything is not all right, but also no, she hasn't touched me. At least not today."

She must have rendered him without reply because he didn't say anything for a moment, and she couldn't bring herself to look at his reaction.

"I'm beginning to wonder if Daniel and I are an ill-fitted match." Her eyes misted at the admission, but her heart echoed one word back at her. *Truth.* It was the truth, and she had practically driven herself ill trying to bury it.

All night the realization had plagued her, preventing her from slipping into any form of rest. What had started as a simple journey to figure out how to fix the uneasiness she felt over their rushed relationship led to a conclusion she fought the rest of the night to avoid: they were ill-fit.

Maybe at one point she thought the problem in their relationship was from not knowing each other deeply enough, but that wasn't the full truth. She had held back parts of her story, unaccustomed to being open with anyone, but Daniel had never held back any part of himself. Even in the short time they'd known each other, he had been an open book for her to decide how she felt.

The expectations of a future with him were clear. Her role as his wife was already laid out before her, but the more she looked at the outline of what that was, the less certain she was that she wanted it.

"I feel like I'm waking from a dream," she whispered, gripping her skirt in her fists. "Everything glittered so beautifully before. I think I was too blinded by my own expectations to see Daniel for who he is."

Daniel's face filled her mind, his clear blue eyes twinkling with his charming smile. His twin dimples winking at her, tugging her heart. From the moment she first laid eyes on him, she hadn't been able to see anything else besides the dazzling smile and kind heart behind it. He was still kind. He was still a good man, but he was also an heir. That was his life, and all of his dreams and visions for the future centered around that title. He was a social elite, and if she wanted him, she would have to take everything that came with it, including the pressure of the eyes of the public and the expectations of a Prindall bride. She had thought it was a simple matter of learning how to fit into his world, but what if she was a puzzle piece that could never fit? There was nothing wrong with Daniel or the life he wanted. There was nothing wrong with her or the life she had dreamed of, but maybe some things were never meant to go together.

"Are you saying you want to break your engagement?" August broke into her thoughts, his even tone doing little to expose his thoughts.

Evelyn opened her mouth, but the words refused to form. Her heart wrenched at the thought of admitting it. Was she ready to break the engagement? She had loved Daniel for a lifetime, and without him, she was back where she started: under Prudence's roof, without love and clinging only to her prayers that something better would come her way. How could she walk away from the only answer she had?

"I don't know if I can," she choked out past her aching throat. "It feels like too much."

"Have you prayed about it?"

She looked up at his earnest expression. There was no judgment or accusation in his soft gaze. "Without ceasing throughout the night," she admitted.

"In my experience, God leads His answers with peace. Keep listening and follow where the peace leads."

She wrapped her fingers around the cross necklace as she tried to center her thoughts on the prayers she'd prayed through the night. *Where is my peace?* Her mind settled on the only peace she had received in several days, but it wasn't where she expected. When she slipped her three acquisition letters into the post box, nervousness skittered under her skin, but her core remained stable with a strange sense of peace. As if she was doing exactly what she was supposed to.

The thought of someone else reading her words and finding meaning in them brought her a sense of purpose. Was that God's answer? Was that what she was supposed to chase instead of this fantasy with Daniel? But that didn't help her escape her lonely home.

"Can writers support themselves?" she blurted before she could stop herself.

"It's possible." August rubbed the back of his neck. "I've managed to do it, but it takes time to get here. Often you have to write several books before you see a worthwhile profit. Are you considering publishing your story?"

"I already submitted it." She licked her lips before chewing her lower lip. "But I don't know if they'll like it. For all I know, no one will ever want to publish it."

"There are other ways to support yourself until someone picks up your story. I've said it before, I'm sure my sister-in-law would be happy to connect you with homes and job opportunities and anything else—"

"No." She squeezed her eyes shut as her heartbeat roared in her ears. Even though she had entertained the idea for a moment, hearing him talk about it sent a tidal wave of fear over her senses. "How can I do that? I would only be trading one lonely life for another. How could that be an answer to my prayers?"

Tears blurred her vision as desperation tightened her chest. If she thought about marrying Daniel, it overwhelmed her. If she thought about abandoning her lifelong dreams with him, it overwhelmed her. Where was she supposed to turn?

"'For My thoughts are not your thoughts, neither are your ways My ways, saith the LORD.' Sometimes the Lord brings answers in ways we least expect it." August scooped down to pluck a dandelion. He spun it between his fingers, watching the white seeds break free and dance on the breeze over the pond. "There is a third option."

His gaze softened as it traced over her face, and something twisted in Evelyn's belly.

"If it's a marriage you want, you don't have to sit around and wait." He drew each word out as if gauging her reaction before saying the next one.

Her mouth dried as her tongue froze to the roof of her mouth, and her breathing came to a shuddering halt.

"You can just say no." He shoved off the bench to stand, raking a hand over his hair and dislodging it from its stiff position. "You don't have to stare at me like I've grown two heads. I only thought... we've grown fond of each other, haven't we?" With a deep inhale, he turned back to her, his eyes pleading his case. "I think I've finally found my inspiration again, and I'm making plans for my next adventure. I would love to take you with me. You would be far from the influence of your stepfamily, and I promise I will do everything in my power to make you feel happy, comfortable, and loved."

Her shock melted into an emotion she couldn't name the longer he spoke. Warm yet sad at the same time. She closed her gaping mouth.

"August..." Speaking his name with familiarity intensified the twisting in her stomach.

Could she do it? Could she break her engagement with Daniel to live a completely different life with August? It would be thrilling. She would be able to live the adventures she had only ever read about in his books.

"Why do you like me, August?" she murmured. "You barely know me." But that wasn't necessarily true. In the weeks they've known each other, she had poured her heart out to him in a way she never did with anyone else, not even Daniel.

He dropped to one knee in front of her and enveloped her hand in both of his. She couldn't bring herself to pull away from his warm touch. "How could I not? From the moment I introduced myself to you, you haven't stopped showing me your kindness and your intelligence. You have a soft heart, despite your stepfamily's suppression, and patient faith in God. Maybe that's what touched me the most. You brought me back to the light when I thought I was too far gone. Maybe I'm a bit selfish in my feelings. I bared my brokenness to you the last time we met here, and your faith-filled words showed me that my stories still matter to the world and that my time as a writer isn't finished. I want you by my side so that this healing I've found can continue."

Her eyes misted over again. How was it that August had known her the same amount of time as Daniel, yet he saw her in a completely different light?

Daniel was not the man for her. If there were any lingering doubts before, she couldn't hold onto them anymore. She looked into August's earnest expression, his love evident in the depths of his eyes. He might as well have been kneeling with his heart in his hands, extended for her to accept or push away.

"August." She breathed his name again.

He squeezed her hand. "When I said I'd be leaving soon, the truth is I've already contacted my publisher, and we've arranged for me to leave on the first train available in a week, to the Grand Canyon. I reserved two tickets."

Her eyes widened. The roaring in her ears began again, and her fingers started to tremble in his grasp. *Too fast.* It was all too fast. A vision of Daniel filled her mind, his knee on the ground and a ring box in hand. *Too fast.*

"I...can't." She didn't realize the words were coming from her until a shadow of sadness passed over August's eyes, and he released her hand.

She licked her lips, but something inside her stilled. "I can't go with you," she repeated despite the painful twist in her chest.

August was a good man, and he was worthy of her trust. She could believe him if he said he would care for her all of her days, but she couldn't forget about Daniel with the snap of her fingers.

No matter if she was sure about the choice she needed to make or not, it would be cruel to treat the love Daniel offered her with disdain by leaving in the arms of another. It would be cruel to herself. His heart wasn't the only one entangled in this ill-matched engagement. Hers had been entangled for far longer, and picking up the shredded pieces would take time. It would take time to seek God for the answer to the hurt she was feeling and to figure out what He had in store.

"I'm sorry," she whispered.

"Are you sure?" August asked, the sadness in his tone tearing her heart further.

A tear dripped onto her cheek, but she nodded. "I'm sure. Maybe I do need to break off my engagement. Maybe it'll be better for both Daniel and me. I can't be the wife he needs, but I can't turn around and take off with another instead. He would never forgive me. My family would never forgive me. I don't know if I would be able to forgive myself."

"You might be a better person than me, but I'll understand."

As he rose to his feet and turned away, desperation rose in her chest. Was that it, then? Were they finished for good? Her muscles tensed as she resisted the urge to grab his hand to prevent him from walking away.

"I meant what I said." Gruffness marred the emotion in his voice, and he kept his back to her. "Every word, including that I'll understand. I don't want to pressure you into something you don't want. However, should you change your mind in a week, the ticket will be there until the moment the train leaves."

Another tear fell down her face as he clasped his hands behind his back and strode away. She watched his tall form through the blur of her emotions, trying to memorize every part.

Lord, have I made the right choice?

Unable to sit alone on the bench now marked with too many memories shared with August, Evelyn grabbed her book and pushed herself to her feet. Through tear-blurred eyes, she found the gravel path and retraced her steps the same way she arrived. If only August had come into her life at a different time. If only he had come sooner, before she ever went to that ball and met Daniel. Or maybe he should have come much later, long after she had already realized the fallacy of her dreams with Daniel. After she had time to let go and heal.

Why had God brought August into her life when He did? It felt even more cruel than ripping away her hope of a future with Daniel. If she was doing the right thing, could she trust Him to bring August back into her life at a better time? She would have to.

On her walk home, Evelyn hugged the book to her chest. The sun was still as bright as it was earlier, and the world was still as warm. But the warmth didn't reach her core. When she slipped in the back door of her family's home, the obnoxious sound of her stepsisters' loud voices met her. They were arguing over something, but the only words she caught were "hymnal" and "selfish."

She made her way through the house, her steps muted on the hall rugs. She avoided detection up the first staircase, and her stepsisters slammed their bedroom doors with frustrated screams as she passed. At the top of the last staircase, she closed herself into the quiet haven. With a sigh, she fell onto her bed and stared up at the ceiling.

Evelyn lay there for a few minutes, staring at the wooden beams above her bed. In the park, the answer for her and Daniel seemed so clear, but with the fresh pain of her goodbye to August, her confidence wavered. If she left Daniel, it would be a final goodbye to the life she had always dreamed of. A final goodbye to the fairytale she thought would be hers. To the promise of luxury and a comfortable life for the rest of her days. The Prindalls would shun her for sure. Edith may never forgive her.

Would it be worth it? August said she could become a writer, but she hadn't heard from any of the publishing companies. He also believed she could find another job, but would that be enough to fill her lonely life?

"For My thoughts are not your thoughts, neither are your ways My ways, saith the LORD.' Sometimes the Lord brings answers in ways we least expect it."

Was that why God brought August into her life when He did? To give her guidance when she needed it most?

She closed her eyes as she rested her hand over her mother's necklace. "Heavenly Father, have You brought me to this point to show me something better? How can I know You have something better in store if I give up my dream?"

The silence in her room rang in her ears, but she lay still

with her eyes closed. After several minutes of jumbled silent prayers, thoughts began to align. Like a train, Bible verses and lines of hymns sung in church marched through her mind, all pointing to God's goodwill and His guiding hand. With those heavenly thoughts came thoughts about those she loved most in this world. Her papa. Edith. August. Daniel. Her decision would not only affect her. It would change the lives of everyone closest to her.

With her mother's cross grasped in her palm, Evelyn prayed for wisdom and for courage. She prayed that whatever path she chose would help and not hurt those around her. Even if it felt like it hurt for a moment, she wanted to make sure they would be all right in the end. She prayed that somehow God would work things out for His glory and their good.

As the day slipped into fading evening, Evelyn didn't rouse from her room. She remained at her bed in prayer, drawing her Bible near for divine direction and strength. The cross of her mother's necklace pressed grooves into her palm from her relentless grasp. At some point, when evening blackened to night, she drifted off to sleep, but when she woke at the first morning light, her hand still rested on her open Bible.

The moment she became aware of her surroundings, all of the night's turmoil rushed back to her, but before she could dwell on it further, a decisive thought filled her mind.

A dull ache settled in her chest, but the wrestling in her spirit stilled into an odd peace. The exact peace August told her would come.

She squeezed her eyes shut, allowing herself to cry. Her father may lose his promotion. Edith may never speak to her again. She may find herself completely alone in the world. But it was the only right solution for her.

Her gaze drifted to *Peril on the Cliffs of Moher* on her nightstand. A tear trailed down the bridge of her nose. How fitting that this book entered her life at the same time as everything else. And what was the grand conclusion of Howard Knightly's daring story? When he came to the end of all else, trapped on the deadly cliff, Howard took the only option: he leapt off the edge.

Her fears were many. Her questions weren't necessarily answered either, but she couldn't deny the truth any longer. She had nothing left to do but trust in the goodness of God and jump into the unknown, like Howard, believing that He would provide a ledge of safety.

CHAPTER 14

"I will inform Young Master Prindall that you're here, and I'm sure he will be with you soon," the butler promised as he escorted Evelyn to the parlor.

"Thank you." She gave Johnson a nod before sinking into one of the high-backed chairs.

She stared out the large windows at the sprawling green Prindall estate. She reminded herself to breathe to steel her nerves, but for once, her fingers didn't tremble.

"Evelyn, I heard you were here." Edith breezed into the room, a smile on her beautiful face. "More wedding details to discuss with my brother?"

"In a way." Evelyn searched her lifelong friend's face. She didn't want to forget this smile, lest it be the last one she received. *Please, Lord, don't let her hate me.*

Edith's smile faded at Evelyn's expression. "You look as if someone has died. What's the matter?" She sat in the chair next to Evelyn and took both her hands in her own.

Evelyn squeezed Edith's hands, wanting to hold tight while she still could. "Please forgive me for what I'm about to tell you."

"Evelyn, you're scaring me," Edith whimpered.

"I can't marry your brother." A lump formed in Evelyn's throat when the words finally left her mouth. *Truth.*

Edith blinked in shock as if the words couldn't soak in. "Why in heavens not?"

"Because..." Would Edith ever understand? "We're not right for each other, and I think, in time, he would see we're ill-fit too."

"But you love him!" Edith ripped her hands out of Evelyn's grip to cross her arms. "You have always loved him. Now he's falling in love with you too. How can you say you are ill-fit?"

"It's not as simple as feelings." Evelyn hesitated as she searched for a way to explain. "You asked me once what I liked about your brother."

"And you answered with some lame excuse of what's not to love?"

Evelyn smiled past the bittersweet feelings mixing inside. "I remember the first time I realized I loved him. Or I thought I did, at least."

"What are you talking about?"

"Do you remember when Daniel brought Daisy home?"

"Of course. We were having a tea party that was rained out, and his carriage hit Daisy on his way home from school. That's when you fell in love with him?"

Evelyn nodded. "I still remember crouching on the kitchen floor with him as he treated her wounds. I had never seen someone give gentle care to an animal like that. I was only thirteen, but I was certain I wanted to marry that man."

As she returned her gaze to the window, the memory came back like a picture before her eyes. Daniel knelt over the injured puppy, still in his muddy boots and dripping coat. His sandy hair clung to his forehead, rivets of rainwater trailing down his young face. Even as his mother fretted over his health from being soaked in the rain, he focused on the puppy. His gentle fingers washed and bound her wounds the best he could.

When the puppy came to again, he fed her warmed milk from a spoon.

"He was always handsome to me, but at that moment I saw a heart of gold," Evelyn whispered. "In his raincoat and muddy boots, cradling an injured puppy, he wasn't the heir to a great enterprise. He wasn't someone important or out of reach. He was simply a boy who deeply cared for anyone or anything in need, and that's what I fell in love with."

"As much as I joke that he is a dolt, he does have a heart of gold," Edith insisted. "He hasn't cared about your position in life, and he loves you as you are. Doesn't that prove it?"

Evelyn's mind drifted through the memories of the past few days, to the words he said that revealed how little he knew of her. His actions, though unintentional, hurt her deeply. "He's been nothing short of a gentleman to me. He has cared for me the best way he knows how."

"Then where is this coming from? You're making no sense."

Evelyn rubbed her forehead as her heart constricted. "I fell in love with that moment, and it colored how I viewed every-thing else after. I never considered that no matter his heart, he is still an heir. His life is very different from mine, and there's nothing that will change that. No matter how much I care for him or him for me, I must change myself to be with him. I have to be proper, learn all of the nuances in your etiquette, and step into the role of his wife in the public eye. We can't just be the boy with the heart of gold and the girl who adores him. It's not enough. Not for me. Not for him."

"That's such a stupid reason to give up on a life-long love." Edith threw her hands in the air as she flopped back in her seat, frustration laced in each word. "You can learn. I can teach you, and I don't think Daniel cares if you make a couple of mistakes along the way."

"But I don't want it. I used to think all the parties, engage-ments, and society charming, but now... I don't want it. I don't want my every action to be judged. I don't want the pressures of being a hostess and perfect wife. If I succeeded at all the last month to blend into this world, it's not me. It was you. Your lessons, your clothes, your makeover. I loved the dream in my head, but I don't think that dream can become reality without being spoiled."

"Evelyn..."

"Daniel deserves someone who can be a helpmate, not a hindrance." A peace settled over her heart as she wrapped her fingers around her cross necklace. "I love Daniel, and I think my heart will reserve a special place for him until the end of time. But this will be better for both of us."

"You're going to break his heart. I never thought you would do something like this."

Evelyn pressed her eyes closed and lowered her head. "I'm sorry. Please forgive me."

"How could you?" Edith whispered, and when Evelyn forced herself to meet her friend's gaze, she found her baby blue eyes vibrant with tears.

Their gazes held before Edith turned her face away. She opened her mouth as if to say something but then closed it again.

"I'm sorry," Evelyn whispered desperately.

"How can you call yourself my friend?" Edith choked before fleeing from the room.

Tears burned Evelyn's eyes, blurring her vision. Speaking the truth to her friend strengthened her assurance, but that didn't stop the sting of Edith's rejection, surely the first of many. Everyone would think her insane for letting such an opportunity slip through her fingers, and perhaps she was a little insane.

"God, help me," she muttered under her breath as she dried her cheeks and blinked her emotions back into check.

"Evelyn?" Daniel's confused tone drew her gaze to the doorway.

His attention was still over his shoulder, most likely following the path of his sister's stormy exit. The disorder of his appearance the last time she had seen him was erased, and the perfectly composed Daniel she always knew walked toward her.

"Did you and Edith fight?" he asked. "I don't know that I've ever seen you two fight."

"It's my fault," she whispered.

He replaced Edith in the seat next to her, but when he took her hands, she pulled back instead of relishing the contact.

"What's the matter, Evelyn?" Daniel frowned as his hands fell into his lap.

"Daniel, I'm sorry, but I cannot marry you."

He stared at her with the same shocked expression as Edith, and she forced her gaze to hold his. She could only pray it conveyed the remorse she felt.

His nostrils flared as he breathed out, but then he schooled his expression into an even look. "There's no need to jump to rash decisions. What happened to taking a few days off to recover from your stress?"

"This isn't a rash decision. I tried to find any solution other than this, but I can't ignore the truth anymore." She stood, twisting the beautiful engagement ring off her finger. She held the ring out before him, her heart begging him to accept it gracefully. She didn't know if she could withstand anything less. "I can't be a socialite or estate keeper, and I don't want to be. I've tried everything I can to fit into your world, but I don't want to live the rest of my life in a façade."

"Wait, just wait." He took the ring but held it away from himself, staring at it with a twist of confusion and hurt. "What happened the last few days? I thought things were fine. I thought you were learning everything from Edith, and I thought we were happy."

Her tears returned, but this time she didn't stop them from falling. "I don't know how to explain it anymore, but I know that we're not right for each other. We're too different. You love your role as your father's son—as you should—but I value my freedom and privacy too much to be part of it. Sooner or later I would have let you down, and sooner or later it would have become too much for me. I hope, in time, you'll be able to forgive me and see that I was right."

He turned away from her as he rubbed a hand over his mouth. "Do you understand what you're doing to me? To my family? The world will hear I've been abandoned by a factory manager's daughter."

Her heart sank into her stomach, but she couldn't fault him for thinking about that. She understood now that the perception of others mattered in his world, but it only cemented her decision further. She didn't want to live with the weight of the world's opinion on her choices. She chewed on her lip as she tried to think of an answer he might accept.

He pressed his lips in a line as he glanced over his shoulder. "I can't change your mind?"

She dropped her eyes to the ground in a silent answer.

"Then don't ask me to forgive you."

She squeezed her eyes shut, but a tear leaked out of her inner eye. Drawing a deep breath, she willed herself to raise her chin again. "Goodbye, Daniel. I truly am sorry. Thank you for the wonderful dream. I'll never forget it."

He paced to the window, his ridged back to her and his arms crossed. Her ring disappeared in the tight grip of his fist. Realizing there was nothing else she could say, Evelyn started for the exit but paused in the doorway of the parlor. "I brought the trunk of things Edith gave to me. The dresses, the jewelry. If I owe you any more debt, I'll find a way to pay it."

He said nothing, keeping his back to her. Her gaze lingered on his sandy hair one last time before she left. She let herself out of the house before the butler could find her in her emotional state. Instead of hailing a carriage, she walked through town toward home, hoping the air would calm her emotions and clear her head.

No matter how sure she was that this was the right decision, her heart ached like it would break into two as she walked away from everything that had been her lifelong dream. Everything that had been the only future she could ever imagine.

Lord, her mind whispered. *I'm letting go.*

CHAPTER 15

Evelyn paused at the front door of her family's home, staring at the golden knocker. Everything in her wished that breaking the engagement with Daniel was the end of it. That she could retreat into herself to find healing, but her family needed to know. It would be a miracle if Prudence didn't throw her onto the street immediately.

Evelyn closed her eyes as she hugged herself. *Lord, I have no strength left for this.* The only answer to her silent plea was the same sure feeling beneath the aching in her chest, assuring her that she was doing what was right no matter how much it hurt. Before she could give herself any more time to hesitate, she opened the door, and the familiar sound of the pounding piano greeted her.

"Evelyn, is that you?" Prudence called from the sitting room.

Evelyn cleared the emotion from her throat before replying, "Yes, I just returned from seeing the Prindalls."

"It's about time. Go help Lottie finish supper before we waste away!"

Evelyn closed her eyes to draw in a calming breath. After putting her hat on the rack by the door, she hurried down the hall toward the kitchen, but she stopped by her father's ajar study door. Darkness blanketed the shelves of the room, his desk highlighted by a weak beam of light leaking through the doorway. She stared at his empty chair, wishing he would come home early for once. Then she could tell him about her news first and leave him to tell his wife.

Evelyn pulled back, returning the door to its original position. A heaviness weighed her steps as she continued into the kitchen.

"I'm here to help, Lottie," she announced when she entered the warm kitchen, but her tone didn't quite carry the normalcy she hoped.

Lottie looked up from cutting a carrot and frowned. "Miss, what's the matter? You look ghastly."

"You always know how to cheer me." Evelyn failed to produce a genuine smile. "The rest of the family won't know until I announce it at dinner, but I've broken my engagement with Daniel."

Lottie's knife clattered to the cutting board as she stared at Evelyn.

Evelyn dropped her gaze to the wooden floor. "I think I've decided to get a job, find a ladies' home, and make my own way until I can find something better." Her heart balked as the words left her mouth, but she knew there wasn't any other option. She couldn't stay in this house any more than she could marry Daniel.

"And you are sure?"

"Yes," she whispered, forcing herself to meet Lottie's eyes.

Lottie stared at her for a minute more before nodding. "I'll say a prayer for you. Heaven knows you'll need it." She motioned to the oven with her knife. "The meat needs flipping."

She hurried over to do Lottie's bidding, and neither woman said any more about the subject. Evelyn listened for the front door as they worked in unison, but when Lottie dished the steaming pork and sautéed vegetables onto dinner plates, Evelyn's stomach twisted. Upon Lottie's request, Evelyn left the kitchen to set the table while the housekeeper called her family to eat. Her nerves skittered across her skin, sending her heart racing.

She helped Lottie place the food on the table before taking her seat next to her stepmother. Her stepsisters paid her no mind as they spread their napkins in their laps. With her father's chair empty at the head of the table, the meal proceeded without his customary prayer.

Fear gripped her heart, but a bolt of courage forced her chin up. "I'm not going to marry Daniel. I broke the engagement today."

Prudence's fork clattered to her plate as silence enveloped the room. Her stepsister's wide-eyed gazes skittered between their mother and Evelyn.

"This is not a funny joke," Prudence stated, clutching her napkin in a vise grip.

"It's not a joke." Evelyn forced her tone to remain even. "We aren't a good match, and I don't want his life. I plan to find a job and a room at a ladies' home instead. I had hoped Papa would be here—"

"Have you lost your mind?" Prudence's eyes blazed as she slammed her hand on the table. Her pitch rose with every word. "Do you understand what you are doing? Do you understand how that will affect your family? Do you understand how this will affect your father?"

Evelyn closed her eyes before turning to face her stepmother's rage. "I won't do something that I believe is not God's will for me."

"God's will?" Prudence sputtered. "And you believe working like a vulgar hussy and dishonoring not only your entire family, but also Daniel and his family, is God's will? You had better pray it's not too late to undo your disastrous mistake." Prudence bolted to her feet, her chair toppling behind her skirts. "On your feet. You're going to beg on your knees for him to take you back."

Evelyn remained seated as Prudence grabbed her arm. "No, I won't."

Her face became a red mask of rage. Evelyn turned her head away, but not in time to avoid Prudence's open palm to her cheek.

"You ungrateful urchin!" Prudence dragged Evelyn out of her chair. "You've ruined us! You've ruined your father! None of us will be able to show our faces in public again!"

Tears stung Evelyn's eyes, but she managed to twist out of her stepmother's grasp. She scrambled back until her back was pressed against the wall.

"Nothing you say or do will ever change my mind," Evelyn declared, setting her jaw to keep her chin from trembling.

Prudence swung toward her again, but this time Evelyn grabbed her wrist. "Don't touch me."

Evelyn pushed her stepmother's arm away, causing her to stumble.

"How dare you disrespect our mother!" Dahlia screamed.

Before the two sisters could round the table to defend Prudence, a booming voice stopped the commotion in its tracks.

"What is going on?"

Evelyn's gaze flew to the doorway where her father filled the opening. He was still dressed in his homburg hat and overcoat. His mouth hung open as he took in the scene before him, anger storming in his eyes.

Prudence clutched both hands to her chest, her eyes suddenly filled with large tears. "Edwin, oh, Edwin, it's terrible. Your-your wretch of a daughter broke her engagement and has doomed us all. She flew into a rage when I tried to talk her out of it."

"She's gone mad," Dahlia wailed.

He set his jaw as he turned his attention to Evelyn. "Is that true?"

"No!" She clenched her fist. "Well, yes. Yes, I broke my engagement, but I—"

"She's ruined us," Prudence moaned.

Edwin frowned at his wife before focusing on Evelyn. "Why did you do this?"

Before Evelyn could say anything, Prudence stepped forward. "She believes she's on some high mission from God, but she's disgraced us all—"

"That's enough." Edwin sliced his hand through the air. "Evelyn, I want to speak to you in my study. Alone."

Prudence's jaw dropped as he turned on his heels to leave. Shaking with either courage or fear—or perhaps both—Evelyn trailed behind her father, leaving her stepfamily behind in shocked silence.

Upon reaching his office, Edwin shrugged off his overcoat, throwing his hat onto the peg by the door. Evelyn waited by the door as he stalked to his desk, and he kept his rigid back to her, knuckles resting on his desktop. The seconds seemed to tick by with neither of them moving.

"Why?" His question was quiet but firm.

Weary from explaining more times than she could count, her gaze went to the ceiling as she licked her lips. "It wasn't right."

"Daniel would have taken care of you."

"I know," she murmured, gripping her hands in front of her.

"He would have given you whatever you needed to be happy. A million books. A puppy. An international trip. He would have given you more than you could dream."

"His money can't buy what I need to be happy."

His shoulders wilted before he turned to her. "He would have given you a good life."

Evelyn twisted her fingers together, fighting for the right

words. "Monetary comfort does not equal good." When he said nothing, his gaze merely sweeping her face, she squared her shoulders. "I've found something else I believe will be good."

"Another man?" The gruffness returned to his voice.

"A novel," she whispered. "I'm writing a novel about Mother."

"A...novel?" Confusion crossed over his wary expression.

"I used to tell Mother stories as we worked together. She encouraged me to. This is one last story for her, and it's about her. It's not strictly her story since it's fictional, but it contains everything she taught me about faith, love, and goodness. I feel close to her again."

Staring at the ceiling, her father worked his jaw back and forth, swallowing as grief deepened the wrinkles around his eyes.

She forced herself to go on. "In a way, I suppose there is another man, but I'm not leaving Daniel for him. Not in that way. The same week that I went to Edith's party and danced with Daniel, I met my favorite author, August Cates, at our church picnic."

"The adventure author you're always reading? You met him? You never told me about this."

There's a lot you don't know anymore. She bit her lip, holding back those unspoken words. "He's the one who inspired me, and when he read the beginning of my story, he encouraged me to share it with others. At first I thought I never could, but now I want to try. In honor of Mama."

He covered his eyes with his hand, blocking her ability to read his expression. So she stood in silence, waiting for him to give some sign as to whether or not this news further disappointed him.

He wiped his hand down his face as he shook his head, his eyes reddening. "Your mother would be proud of you," he whispered.

She closed her eyes as something burned in her, screaming for him to say the words himself. That *he* was proud of her too.

"But Daniel," he spoke up again. "I'm sure he would have supported you. One novel is hardly reason enough to throw away an entire life."

Evelyn's shoulders tensed, but she forced herself not to shrink away. "It wasn't right, Papa. We would have both ended up unhappy. I can't sentence myself to a life with someone I know isn't right."

He turned slightly as he pinched the bridge of his nose, and she bit her lip, wishing she had picked different words.

"I do have a plan for my life," she promised. For the third time that morning, she found herself explaining her plan to provide for herself. Except this time her words faltered, and each sentence was harder than the last. Somehow, telling her father seemed like the final nail in the coffin. She was leaving everything she knew in hopes of finding something better.

Was better even possible?

"So, I'll be leaving as soon as I'm able," she murmured.

Another painful silence enveloped them as he massaged his forehead, his face crinkled into an expression she couldn't fully understand. Was he angry? Sad? Regretful?

"Evelyn, I'm sorry I…" He shook his head as he worked his hands over his face. "When I remarried, I never intended for… By the time I realized…" He clenched his fist by his side, his gaze returning to the ceiling as he released a long, shaking breath.

"Do you love Prudence?" Evelyn whispered.

"I thought I was doing what would be best for all of us."

"Did you ever love her?"

"You needed a mother. We needed a lady of the house. I thought sisters would keep your childhood from being too lonely. I thought being a big family would fill this house with life again. I thought…" His strangled words faded off as he turned his back to her.

Evelyn's gaze traced over his hunched shoulders, and for the first time, she saw the dark shadow that had eclipsed her father since her mother's death for what it was.

When she lost her mother, everyone, including her father, gave her room to grieve. They permitted her to cry. To curl up with her mother's old dresses, clinging to their fabric like she used to cling to her. They let her keep mementos and follow through the steps of grief until it faded into something manageable and not as sharp.

Had anyone given her father room to grieve? Even after losing his wife, he was still a factory manager, a father, a man with numerous responsibilities resting on his shoulders. His days had marched on, no room to wait for grief to run its course.

She dropped her gaze to the rug, and the expanse between them seemed all the more dark and yawning. How many years had they lost in their relationship because of his choices after her mother's death? How much hurt had he heaped on her by simply not being around? He could have made different choices. He could have changed the outcome. Life could have been different if he had simply done things differently.

But how many of his thoughtless actions over the years were him simply trying to dull the pain? Mask it?

She turned, looking to the door. He had made his choices, and she needed to make hers. Neither of them could change the past, but her future wasn't set in stone. She stepped toward the door, but her heart wrenched, freezing her feet.

"You think other people would fix my happiness. I was already happy." She closed her eyes as an image of her papa filled her mind. Young. Smiling. Welcoming. "I've never needed anything other than what you already gave me. You were enough."

"Evelyn..."

"I'm sorry I have to leave," she whispered. "I can't stay."

"Go. I won't stand in your way. Go find what God has for you."

Evelyn surrendered her feet to her heart, and she found herself crossing the space between them. She wrapped her arms around his middle, and when he opened his arms in surprise, she rested her head on his shoulder.

After a heartbeat, his arms enveloped her and held her tight. "I'm sorry, Evelyn. I'm so sorry."

She couldn't say anything more as tears raced down her cheeks onto his shirt. He rested his cheek on her hair, and she felt his tears too. The hurt aching at the edges of her emotions reminded her of the years built on offenses between them, but she focused on something else that was beginning to warm her core. She held him tighter, knowing this might be the last time for a while.

"I have no right to ask anything of you, but will you promise me one thing?" her father asked into her hair.

She nodded against his shoulder, her throat too tight to speak.

"Let me read your story. When it's done or when it's published. Whichever you are most comfortable with."

She lifted her head to look into his glistening gaze. "Of course."

Cupping her face in his hands, he pressed a kiss to her forehead. "A spitting image of your mother, complete with her courage. I'm proud of you."

Evelyn's chin trembled as she stepped away from her father and walked toward the door. She paused in the doorway, her tear-blurred gaze roaming the small study to commit every inch, every smell, every sensation to memory. Her father rested one hand on his desk as he wiped his face with the other, his shoulder turned toward her.

"I love you, Papa," she whispered before slipping out.

Emotion weighed Evelyn's feet as she passed through the

hall and up the stairs of her childhood home. Every step brought a mirage of memories, leaving the sound of her mother's laugh and her father's rich voice in her ears.

She came to stand in the doorway of the attic room that had become her haven when her stepfamily came. She gazed around at the ramshackle furniture. Years ago she had sacrificed her bedroom for her new "sisters," and every year following she had sacrificed her own desires to bend to the will of her overbearing stepmother. All for the sake of her father. To take a weight off his shoulders, yet she realized now she was never the weight that bent his spirit.

She crossed the room to open the trunk at the foot of her bed so she could pack. The trail of heartache and hard choices she had put herself through in the last twenty-four hours pressed on her, but she forced herself to fold and tuck away her dresses instead of letting the emotion swallow her.

"Go find what God has for you."

Her father's voice echoed through her mind as she sank to sit next to her full trunk. The unknown of the future stretched before her like a threatening void. She couldn't picture what life on her own would be like. She still wasn't sure that she wouldn't hate it, but as she wrapped her hand around her mother's necklace, her heart whispered, *"Leap."*

CHAPTER 16

 velyn sat at the desk in the room she was still learning to call hers. The mail lay abandoned on the desk, but she couldn't bring herself to flip through it or hold out the hope that Edith or August's names might be on one of the envelopes. She couldn't bring herself to do anything but sit and feel the tight ache at the base of her neck spreading into her shoulders from bending over her work all day. Her fingertips rested against her wool skirt, but even that was almost painful to her raw skin, blistered from using a typewriter she wasn't accustomed to.

She closed her eyes as a ripple of laughter leaked underneath her bedroom door, a reminder that it felt like she was the only one in her housing facility who didn't know anyone else. It was her own fault for spending most of her evenings in her room instead of the common rooms where others talked and played games, but after a long day at a job that she was still adjusting to, she couldn't muster the courage required to face a room full of new faces.

As the laughter faded, the silence of her room became an audible ringing in her ears. Her gaze drifted to the bed parallel to hers on the other side of the room, the mattress bare. Everything in the room—the desk, bed, and wardrobe—had a matching twin on the other side of the room, but the set was void of any personal effects.

The solace had been nice for the first couple of days while she settled in, but now the emptiness mocked her. The aching in her body sunk deeper until it radiated from the center of her chest.

Tears filled her eyes. She was so tired. So, so tired. But she was also so lonely. So unbearably lonely. She wanted the comforting presence of someone familiar with whom she could share her woes about her difficult day. Someone who would sympathize as she told of how a man at work got mad at her for not knowing how to type a certain form, but she didn't know because no one had bothered to show her.

Evelyn's gaze wandered around her room. It was bright from the two tall windows on the outside wall, and it smelled of fresh wood stain and clean linens. Somehow she found herself wanting nothing more than her dusty attic room, musty and filled with the familiar broken remnants of her parents' furniture.

Her stomach let out a deep, rumbling gurgle, but she didn't want the mass-prepared food served in the dining room. She wanted a warm roll, fresh from the oven and eaten atop a kitchen barstool beside Lottie's comforting presence.

Evelyn pressed a hand to her mouth as the strong wave of homesickness blurred her vision with tears. Not for the first time in the last couple of weeks, she asked herself if she had made the right decision.

It seemed right before. She had even managed to find a job and this ladies' home within a week of breaking her engagement with Daniel. It seemed like everything fell into place, leading her away from her childhood home and the life she had always known.

The certainty that God was leading her on a different path than what her family and Daniel paved for her had carried her from her childhood home with her head held high. She was a twentieth-century adventurer, embarking on a journey to a world previously unknown.

Evelyn crossed her arms on the desk and buried her face as her sobs began to shake her body, releasing all of her carefully held-together emotions and exhaustion. How had her trust in God's seemingly good plan eroded so quickly?

You made me give up my fairytale ending for this. Why?

When the tears trickled to a stop on her cheeks, Evelyn turned her head to rest her cheek on her arm, staring at the abandoned mail on her desk.

A small spark from somewhere inside of her incited her to move one hand to splay the letters so she could see each return address, her blurry gaze searching for the familiar names she longed for. Maybe if Edith reached out to say she finally forgave Evelyn, or maybe if August had sent a simple note letting her know he had found full healing for his writing, it would be enough for her to pick her head up for another day and keep going.

But neither of their names were on the letters.

Evelyn left her hand resting on the mail, feeling that small spark flickering out again, but her gaze landed on the bottom letter.

Riveting Publishing House

Evelyn raised her head, blinking to make sure she read correctly. Shoving aside the other mail, she picked up the letter to see it had originally been addressed to her family's home, but someone had added a note to forward it to her ladies' home. Lottie? Papa?

Evelyn held her breath as she ripped into the letter, willing herself to hold onto hope and not give in to the doubts that it would only be a rejection letter for her story.

Dear Ms. Macaree,

Thank you for your submission to our publication. We found the story you submitted enchanting, and we would like for you to submit the rest upon its completion.

Evelyn blew out a breath as she reread the first two sentences of the letter. Her gaze flew to her abandoned journal on the corner of her desk, where it had sat untouched for several days. The exhaustion and stress of her days had snuffed out any hope for inspiration, but Rose Wheelock's story still waited between the leather cover, tantalizingly close to its climax but still void of that satisfying conclusion.

A fresh wave of tears rushed to her eyes, but this time they came with a rush of something that almost felt like relief. She blinked the tears back so she could read the rest of the letter. The editor who wrote on behalf of the publishing house went on to discuss the potential he saw in her story and how he could see it becoming a serial for one of their popular magazines. It ended with a repeated invitation to send more of the story and a suggestion to meet in person to discuss edits and other details.

Evelyn wiped at the tears flowing down her cheeks as she skimmed the letter over and over again. Someone loved her story. Someone wanted to bring it to the rest of the world.

Evelyn drew the journal across the desk and flipped open the cover to read the first sentence of her story that introduced Rose Wheelock. A feeling she couldn't identify swirled in her chest, overshadowing every ache from before. Someone was willing to believe in the importance of her mother's story as much as she did.

"I believe in the heart I see in your writing. Someone out there needs your story."

She let out a blubbering laugh through her tears as August's words swept through her memory.

Lord, is this Your answer?

Evelyn took a deep, calming breath as she tried to rein in her whirling thoughts to consider what she needed to do. She needed to finish the story, write it all out as a clean copy for the publisher, and write them back to set up an appointment to speak with the editor. Perhaps her boss at work would allow her to use the typewriter at her desk on a day off or after hours to make a nice copy of her story.

Evelyn propped the acceptance letter on the back of her desk against the wall where she could see it clearly. Then she settled her journal in front of her, turning to where she had left off in the story.

This didn't fix the loneliness. Or the discomfort of learning a new job. Or the intimidation of making a home out of a foreign place.

But her spirit took flight at the clear sign of hope. Maybe this was another piece of God's good plan, and maybe in time, she would see more of the picture He was painting.

CHAPTER 17

With a prayer, Evelyn sealed the envelope containing the next chapter of her story. It was her habit now to send off each new piece of her writing with a prayer for God to use it as He saw fit.

"Evelyn, have you seen this?" Her roommate gasped from where she lay across her bed.

"Hm?" Evelyn glanced over her shoulder to see her roommate reading the society column. "What is the scandal today?"

Adelaide scrambled off the bed to show Evelyn the headline. "Isn't this that man you've talked about?"

Evelyn took the newspaper into her own hands to read the headline: *Daniel Prindall to Marry Oil Heiress!* She scanned the story, a mix of emotions swirling over her. The article summarized the impending nuptials as the result of a "whirlwind romance written in the heavens." She tried not to roll her eyes at the sensational language and handed the paper back to her roommate.

"Edith told me about her. She seems like a sweet girl, but Edith failed to tell me how serious things were becoming." Evelyn turned back to her desk and paused.

Daniel was getting married.

It wasn't exactly sadness she felt. She had nothing to be sad about. She certainly wasn't going to marry him, and he deserved every happiness. But this felt like the official closing of the dream of her adolescence, which brought about a bittersweet feeling.

"Are you all right, Evelyn?" Adelaide whispered. "I know you cared deeply for him."

Evelyn turned a genuine smile over her shoulder. "Yes, I'm happy that he found someone to love. She will be good for him."

She stood from her desk and gathered her mail and journal. "We're both happy now. We're far better off than we would have been together."

"But you're still alone. Doesn't that make you depressed?" Adelaide sighed as she wilted onto her bed. "It would be enough to make me to stay in bed for days."

"I'm blessed, and I couldn't ask for anything more than I have now." She slipped a few spare coins from her bag into the jar on her desk labeled *Adventure Fund*. Her gaze lingered on the letters and postcards lined up on her desk, all little notes and messages from people touched enough by her story to write her. Her heart warmed looking at them.

Adelaide studied her with a skeptical look. "If you say so."

Evelyn laughed as she made her way to the door, grabbing her straw hat off the hook on the wall. "If you knew the life I had before this, you would understand. I'll be back later."

Adelaide snapped her newspaper open. "See you then."

Evelyn descended the stairs of the ladies' home to the main room. Groups of girls lounged around on the various couches and chairs, their chatter filling the room. She waved as she passed through toward the front door, but a package in her mail cubby caught her eye. Pulling the package out, she saw her father's name on the return address line.

She held the brown paper package in her hands, testing the

weight to guess what he might have sent her. Too heavy to be a box of Lottie's baked goods. Too small to be the hat she had been staring at for two weeks in a shop window on her way to and from work. Was it possible it was the right size for a book?

Deciding it was best to open it in private, Evelyn tucked the package into her leather bag and continued out the front door. After pausing on the front step to pin the straw hat securely in her curls, Evelyn pulled her bicycle onto the sidewalk from where it rested beside the building. She draped the bag on the handlebars and settled her skirts over the low bar of the bicycle before pushing off the sidewalk.

The warm wind of late spring tickled the hairs framing her face, and the sun peeked out at her from behind white clouds as she navigated the street traffic.

The bright weather matched the joyful feeling in her spirit, and as she rode down the cobbled street, she couldn't help but let her mind drift over the last year at her new home. Maybe it took a while to get to where she was now, but she wasn't lying when she told Adelaide she was blessed. Somehow God had managed to work good into a life that she never thought could contain hope. Into a job she finally felt confident in, that gave her the money she needed to keep a roof over her head. Into a home she now found comfort in, surrounded by friends she had made. Into restored relationships. Into freedom. Into the coins that built up in her adventure jar, a promise to herself to see the world someday.

After pausing at a mailbox to drop her story, Evelyn steered into the park she frequented so often that she thought of it as *her* park. Sprouts of green grass invaded the cracks of the well-worn path, growing in the patches of light piercing through the new leaves of the large maple oak trees, and squirrels rooted in the foliage for the last of their stashes from the winter.

Evelyn pulled her bicycle up behind her usual bench, happy to see it unoccupied. After retrieving her bag from the handlebars, she sat in the center of the bench. Sunbeams winked at her off the glistening water, and the familiar smell of algae danced on the light breeze.

Unable to contain her curiosity any longer, Evelyn grabbed the mysterious package from her bag and tore into the brown wrapping paper. The paper ripped off the top half of the package, revealing unmistakable gold lettering that spelled out a tantalizing title: *Adventure at the Canyon's Edge.*

Evelyn carefully removed the rest of the paper until the full cover was exposed. Howard Knightly stood on dusty ground, the Grand Canyon visible in the distance behind him, but his focus was on the dark-haired girl in his arms.

Evelyn's gaze traced the author's name written in the same gold as the title. *August Cates.*

She let out a long breath as a strong wave of emotion crashed over her, and she raised her eyes to stare into the pond. August had done it. He finished another book despite his claims a year ago that he may never write again.

The image of a man never far from her dreams surfaced in her mind. A soft smile. Searching eyes. Carefree hair. The only part of her life that didn't feel settled. A man she couldn't seem to go even a day without thinking of. She had let go, never showing up at the train the day it left despite the tugging of her heart. She had trusted God to bring him back to her if it was right, but that didn't stop her heart from wondering if he was well, if his travels would ever bring him back to Boston, if he still thought of her.

She brushed her thumb over the image of Howard and his companion. Had he found a lass on the prairies of the West? Had he forgotten about her existence entirely?

Evelyn cracked open the stiff cover. She closed her eyes, lifting the book to her nose to enjoy the smell of fresh paper, ink, and book-binding glue. When she opened her eyes again, she found a small note tucked inside the cover.

Dear Evelyn,

I hope you haven't already bought this book for yourself. It always brought me joy to buy you these Howard Knightly books and to see the excitement they brought you. I wanted to bring that excitement once again. See you for dinner soon.

Love,

Papa

Evelyn smiled and kissed the card over her papa's signature, his simple note bringing back the warmth of the beautiful day. She tucked the note near the back of the book so she could use it as a bookmark, and then she flipped through the beginning pages until a jarring sight stilled her fingers.

To Evelyn, without whom this book never would have come to be.

She stared at the printed dedication on the page before the first chapter, expecting the words to morph before her eyes, but even when she blinked, they remained the same. She brushed her thumb over the simple dedication. He hadn't forgotten her.

Chewing on her lip, she turned to the next page to begin the new story, and some sort of nervous excitement boiled in her belly. Her own story sat forgotten in the bag next to her, waiting for its next installment. Everything else in the world around her faded away as she followed Howard as he returned to the ranch he once called home, battered and exhausted from all of his grand adventures. Of course, his hope for peace and healing didn't last for long as Dr. Draper tracked down his location to exact his revenge over his ruined flying machine. Despite the distraction of Dr. Draper, a certain dark-haired young woman now employed on his family's ranch caught Howard's eye, stirring in his heart a desire for something he never knew he needed before.

No matter how hard she tried to picture the blond, blue-eyed hero, a certain persistent face remained in her mind's eye as she read page after page, chapter after chapter.

The shadows of the trees shifted around her spot on the

bench as she sat unmoving. Someone slid onto her bench, breaking Evelyn's undivided focus. She blinked up from the pages of the book to see who was bold enough to invade her quiet spot.

"Evelyn."

She stared into his brown eyes as his warm voice sent a shock down her spine. His smile lifted one corner of his mouth.

"What do you think of the improvements?" His gaze dropped to the book in her lap.

"August," she breathed as she gripped the book, her finger serving as a bookmark so she didn't lose her place. He looked exactly as she remembered. Same searching expression. Same carefree hair. Same gentle smile. Though perhaps his tan had grown even darker with the sun.

"I can't tell you how many times I've walked this park over these last few days, hoping I'd run into you. I was beginning to think you had changed your mind and married the stiff heir after all, but the headline this morning calmed my worries." August raised a newspaper in his hand.

"You're here. In Boston." She cringed. Was that the most intelligent thing she could come up with? But his words left her head reeling. He had been searching for her for days?

His smile widened, the corners of his eyes softening. "I'd like to say it's because I finished my newest book, and I'm taking a respite before jumping into the next. But that wouldn't be the full truth. I'm afraid there's someone here I couldn't forget about, and I had to see if she felt the same."

The vulnerability that swept over his expression squeezed at her heart, but her shock kept her frozen in place.

He dropped his gaze to the ground, tapping the newspaper on his thigh. "I'm sorry. It's been so long, and you turned me down once. I only wanted to know if you were well. Are you?"

"I'm very well," she choked out. "I'm free now. And I'm happy. And I'm sharing my mother's story with the world."

"I know." He rubbed the back of his tanned neck with a sheepish look. "I've been keeping up with the serial. I'm still waiting to figure out how this story ends. I've been waiting over a year now."

Evelyn's gaze dropped to the expanse on the bench between them, words failing her again. She wanted to reach out and touch him. Brush her fingers over his. Something to tell herself that he was, in fact, sitting before her in the flesh, but she feared if she did he would evaporate into mist. How many times had she dreamed this moment only to wake up?

"You truly came back for me?" she whispered, the space between them calling for nothing more.

"Truly." He brushed her cheek with his fingertips, sending a rush of tingles through her skin. "I couldn't forget you. I think I may never, but if I can be so bold as to say, I don't think I ever want to."

"August." She breathed his name as she dared to meet his gaze again. "I was praying you would come back when the timing was right."

"How is the timing now?"

Instead of trying to come up with a verbal response, she closed the gap between them. With her eyes closed, she pressed her lips to his. Rather than evaporating into mist, he slipped his hand behind her head and returned the kiss.

As warmth soaked through her entire being, a new path with more unknowns opened in her mind, but no fear followed. She could let God handle the direction of her future with August in her life. She just wanted to enjoy the leap.

ACKNOWLEDGMENTS

Writing is often considered a solitary pursuit, and in a lot of ways, it is. However, this book wouldn't be in your hands today if I'd been alone in this journey. I have a lot of important people to thank for this little story seeing the light of day.

First, I want to thank my parents for all of their support in my writing journey. From buying me the One Year Adventure Novel curriculum for my freshman year of high school to helping me get to writing workshops, they helped me grow in my writing early on. They've always been my encouragers, listening to all of my writer-ramblings, and my mom has lent invaluable aid in proofreading every random thing I've plopped in her hands. Mom and Dad, I truly wouldn't be where I am or the person I am without your love and godly example.

I also want to thank my sister, Brooke, for becoming the most enthusiastic cheerleader of this story. After being an unofficial alpha reader, her love of the story helped me never lose hope in its potential. And, Brooke, thank you for putting up with your quirky writer of a sister for so many years. (That was probably a full-time job of its own.)

I want to thank Ellana, my reader, encourager, idea-bouncer, and dearest friend. I'm pretty sure she was involved in almost every stage of writing this novella from brainstorming to lending me her opinion on the book cover. She never failed to help out whenever I would say "Hey, can I get your opinion on this?" Ellana, throughout my journey in writing, your sweet words have given me courage, and I thank God for your influence in my life over the years.

I can't forget to thank my wonderful editor, Caitlin Miller. Not only did her edits polish my story, but her sweet personal comments inserted in between her edits gave me a boost as I fought to bring this story to its full potential.

Thank you also to my beta readers, Beverly and Megan, for providing valuable feedback on the story.

Megan, thank you for stepping up to help a stranger on the internet with her little novella. Your thoughts on Evelyn's relationship with her father caused me to take a long hard look at the conclusion of their story, and it led me to rewrite the final scene between them in a way that I think elevated the story even more. I truly appreciate the time you took to read my story!

Bev, agreeing to be a beta reader meant the world to me, but you influenced this story far beyond that. Truth be told, this book might not be in the hands of readers without your influence. God used your words in small group to give me courage. When I felt stuck, unsure of what God had for my future, you encouraged me to take a small step where God already had me, and that simple advice led to me making the bold decision to publish this book. Thank you for being a godly source of advice and encouragement in my life in this season!

This story has been years in the making, so I know there have been others along the way who influenced my journey in some way or another. My heart overflows with gratitude for the way God has orchestrated the publishing of this book. I decided years ago to dedicate my writing to bring glory to God, and I see the evidence of His authorship throughout the process. He led me every step of the way, whispering in my ear to have courage when fear said to give up. At the base of it all, it was His faithfulness that inspired me to write this story encouraging others to trust God's good plan for their lives. He is a more perfect Author for our lives than we could ever be.

Last (but far from least), thank you to you, the reader, who has decided to read my little story. I've dreamed of my stories landing in the hands of readers since I was nine years old, and without you, this dream never would have come true. God bless!

Snow
and the
Seven
Brothers'
Circus

Coming soon...

CHAPTER 1

*E*ven thirty feet above the earth, the energy thrumming through the tent swelled to ignite the anticipation in Snow's chest. The cheers of the crowd drowned out the booming words of the ringmaster below, and performers decked in a dazzling array of colors and fabrics exited the ring to allow full attention on the aerial act. Before she could peek at the crowd, the swinging spotlights blinded Snow from seeing anything below, but she didn't need to see them to feel the weight of a thousand eyes on her. Squaring her shoulders, she turned her focus on the only attention she needed for the next few minutes. He waited for her across the expanse of air, his smile beckoning her to leave the platform and fly.

And she did.

As every muscle strained to arch her body through the air, the repetitious music from the bandstand below matched the beat of her racing heart. Halfway across the dizzying void, she released her fingers from the trapeze bar. For a brief, heart stopping moment, she felt nothing but the electric air around her.

Then strong hands wrapped around her wrists, anchoring

her to safety once more, and she looked up into a smile that made everything else fade away. Riding on the raising roar of the crowd, she swung in the security of his grasp. Transferring from his hands by hooking her legs over the next waiting bar, thrill carried her into the next death-defying move with no regard for aching muscles or tiring stamina.

Every fiber of her being glided on the wings of euphoria.

CATHERINE'S EYES FLICKERED OPEN, HER EARS RINGING WITH cheers from a fading dream, but as the colorful image disappeared, the dull darkness of her room settling over her. Her wardrobe, vanity, and bookcases stood around the perimeter of the room like sentinels gazing down on her prone position. The stillness of the air gave the large room an empty feeling, like a body with no soul, and the silence left a hum in her ears.

Catherine tried to shift on the mattress, but the soft filling enveloped her body with an unrelenting hold. Her small form was weighed down with a heaviness that made her limbs feel foreign.

Her gaze drifted to the gray curtains over the two floor-to-ceiling windows. A small strip of sunlight peeked out from under the hem of the curtain, beckoning her to get up and welcome in the beautiful new day. As she stared at the glimpse of light, something stirred in her weary spirit, bidding her to raise from the bed and throw open the curtain, but she could feel that her muscles had given up before the day had even begun.

A soft knock drew her attention away from the window. Without a response, the maid opened the door and slipped into the dark cavernous bedroom. Clutching a tray of food to her middle, the maid drew near to the large four-poster bed with hesitating steps, and Catherine frowned when the girl came close enough for her to see that she wasn't the same maid who tended her the day before.

"I-I'm here to deliver your breakfast, ma'am," the girl's quivering voice broke the silence of the stale room.

She avoided Catherine's eyes as she held the tray up for Catherine to see the meager assortment of bland food. Toast with barely enough butter to soften the dark brown surface. A single hard-boiled egg. A meager bowl of chunky applesauce.

"Thank you," Catherine whispered with a husky voice that sounded strange to her own ears.

Catherine tried to push herself upright, but her arms shook from the effort. Before she could get far, the maid set the tray at the foot of the bed and hurried to her side. The maid couldn't be any older than her own twenty years, but somehow Catherine felt like an ancient crone as the girl supported her back with one arm and drew her pillows up with the other.

"Thank you," Catherine echoed her previous phrase as she sank into her pillows again.

The maid offered a fleeting smile before fetching the tray from the foot of the bed. With tenderness and care as if she was afraid one wrong touch may harm Catherine, she settled the tray on Catherine's lap and assisted her in unfolding the napkin to drape over her nightgown.

Folding her hands politely in front of her, the maid drew back two steps. "Is there anything else I can assist you with?"

Catherine motioned toward her covered windows. "I'd like to see the sunlight. It must be a beautiful day."

The maid hesitated, her gaze darting to the window. Her mouth opened for a moment before she snapped it shut, gripping her hands together. "I... Mrs. Combs gave me strict instructions not to disturb the curtains. She told me that the sunlight wouldn't be good for your condition. She doesn't want it to drain your energy or bring about a headache."

Catherine set her jaw and stared into the applesauce on her

tray. "It can't put me in any worse condition than I already am," she muttered through her teeth.

"P-pardon?" The maid drew one step closer and inclined her ear to listen.

Closing her eyes, Catherine flicked her wrist. "Never mind. That will be all."

The timid maid practically fled the room, and it wasn't until the door clicked shut behind her that Catherine realized she never asked for the girl's name. Maybe it was for the best. Most didn't last long enough for Catherine to make any sort of acquaintance.

Catherine picked up her spoon to stir at the applesauce, but the sight of her own soft, bony hand soured whatever appetite she had. Dropping the spoon, she turned her palms upward. Flickering images from her memory returned, memories of strength that once coursed through her muscles. Of callouses that once marked the base of her fingers.

Catherine pushed the tray further down her legs. Tilting her head back on the pillows, she closed her eyes. She tried to conjure up the colorful, dazzling images of her dreams, but only broken snippets of incomplete memories flickered behind her eyelids.

An ache filled her chest with a longing to return to the times of yesteryear, if just for a moment. To a time where she basked in the sunlight and laughed with a youthful joy. Perhaps those days were short-lived themselves, but it was the one time in her life that everything felt right.

She laid still, beckoning sleep to take her under so that at least in one form or another, she could return. As she drifted to sleep, a smiling gaze surfaced once more in her mind, and she stretched her hand toward him.

A TWENTIETH CENTURY SNOW WHITE RETELLING

Blinding spotlights.
Roaring cheers from an adoring crowd.
Every fiber of her being gliding on the wings of euphoria.

Upon her twenty-first birthday, Catherine Penner is set to inherit her late parents' vast estate and thriving mining business, if she can survive to see the day. An undiagnosed wasting disease threatens to steal her life, leaving her parents' legacy in the hands of her cold guardian.

Fighting to hold onto hope in the face of her own demise, Catherine reflects on the one bright spot in her life after her parents' passing. Like another lifetime altogether, Catherine remembers a time when she was known by a different name. A time when she found belonging and purpose at the Seven Brothers' Circus. But even those beautiful memories come with painful reminders of what's been stolen from her.

As Catherine wrestles with her fragile health and the hopeless meaning of her short life, it soon appears that something sinister is playing with her future. Will she find enough hope to push through to a promising future or will her life fade away like her beautiful memories?

ABOUT THE AUTHOR

Megan Miles's biggest passion centers around creating character-driven historical fiction with themes reflecting God's grace. After penning her first story at nine-years-old, writing became an unstoppable habit that has filled her free time and her dreams ever since. When she isn't writing or working, she has a tendency to volley between every hobby under the sun, including reading, sewing, growing succulents, and playing with her dog.

For more information about her books and to stay updated with the latest news through her newsletter, visit meganmile sauthor.com.

facebook.com/mmiles.writer
instagram.com/mmiles.author

www.ingramcontent.com/pod-product-compliance
Lightning Source LLC
Chambersburg PA
CBHW061541310726
48972CB00008B/2558